The Reader's Circle

C.J. Ward

ISBN: 978-1-312-10251-4

DEDICATION

This book is dedicated to all those who believed in me and offered genuine support throughout my life. Specifically, my mother, Yvonne D. Ward. Thank you for the unconditional love during the twenty-three years I had you on this earth.

CONTENTS

ACKNOWLEDGMENTS

Coming up in the small town of Paducah, Kentucky I learned a great deal about the simple treasures of life. I unfortunately learned a great deal about hard times and hatred as well. With every adversary there were also other individuals that lent their support and motivated me to continue to pursue my dreams. This special group of people are comprised of my immediate family, extended family, close family friends, my church family, a small circle of friends and associates, and a very small number of teachers prior to college. It is in dedication to these individuals in which I write this acknowledgement.

Although I was born in Bowling Green, KY, and raised in Paducah, KY, the extent of my outlook reaches much further than the confines of a "bluegrass" frame of mind. My extensive athletic background has led me to venues from the Atlantic coastline all the way to the Pacific, and as far south as Santiago, Chile. In pursuit of higher education, I had the opportunity to learn and explore various walks of life in Fayetteville, AR and Austin, TX; and eventually made my way back across the state line of Kentucky to Louisville, KY. Regardless of where I resided, there was always one commonality…either chase your dreams or become stagnate in the comfort of not taking chances. Personally, I believe everyone should chase their dreams as if their life depends on it. I believe in it so much so that it inspired me to write this book.

I would like to thank every individual who chose to pick up this literary work for your willingness to read and receive it, and hopefully it will offer inspiration to at least one facet of your life.

Much brotherly love!

C.J. Ward

(Left to Right) James Waters, Eric Thomas, Chris Dunn, Lewis Porter, Frank Neely

PROLOGUE

There was a group of friends; me (James Waters, or 'Jay' for short), Frank Neely, Lewis Porter, Chris Dunn, and Eric Thomas. We all came from the small town of Piedmont, and we had been friends since birth; mainly, because our parents attended the same church. Eric and I were the "loners" of the group when we weren't all together. Chris was well known by everyone for his participation in sports. Lewis had lots of friends and associates (or "homeboys" as he would often refer to them) that were usually viewed at as a problem or trouble. Frank had lots of friends of friends that were girls. Unfortunately for him most viewed his as a brother as opposed to a love interest. From kindergarten, Eric and I seemed to be in the higher-achieving classes, while Lewis, Chris, and Frank were in the lower of the two brackets. But when we were together the thought of us being in different classes would have never crossed your mind. We had a lot of the same experiences and circumstances, and this bonded us. This continued until the first day of school our 6th grade year, when I was sitting in my homeroom class and heard about my school starting a reading club for all grades. The announcement informed that the registration for this club was scheduled to take place immediately following school on that particular day. Needless to say, I was excited about signing up for this reading club for the remainder of the school day; so when the sixth period bell sounded I grabbed my backpack and ran as fast as I could to sign up. When I arrived, I noticed the math teacher I had for 1st grade (*then subsequently had her as a math teacher in the 4th grade as well; which was the pits!!!*) was there with my 6th grade English teacher. Although it struck a certain cord with me, I tried not to pay any attention to it and continued to wait in line patiently until the time came for me to volunteer my signature. After sign-ups, they held a brief introduction about the program and how glad they were that we expressed an interest.

James Waters

Part 1: Childhood

1 THE INITIATIVE

"James, why did you sign up for this club?" my English teacher, Ms. Jasper, questioned as we were being dismissed.

I was quite taken aback by the question but after taking a moment to think about it I replied, "I like to read and I like to learn, that's why I want to be a part of the reading club."

While taking the time to ensure that she looked directly into my eyes after sliding her thick reading glasses slightly down her seemingly long nose, she said, "I don't think you'll be able to join the reading club because Ms. Rash and I don't feel that you really fit the umm.... 'type' to be in this group."

To understand my disdain for these teachers I must give you a little history. I will begin with Ms. Rash (*nick-named by my peers and myself as "the Redheaded Witch of the North" – because she lived in the northern section of town*). She stood about 5'4" in height, with a roly-poly body frame, long thin red hair, and wore big circular-framed glass that seemed to shrink her beady eyes giving her the resemblance of a mouse. Ms. Rash happened to be the first teacher, and only teacher, I had ever flashed a middle finger (*better known as flipping someone the bird*); mainly because of the disapproval for the way she talked to me and my peers. For some reason, she always seemed to offer more hostility towards those who shared the same brown skin pigment as me; so much so, that even the Caucasian students in my class recognized it.

As for Ms. Jasper, this was my first time having her as a teacher; but it certainly wasn't our first meeting. I first met her last school year while running errands for my 5th grade teacher Ms. Moore. I was dropping off a bundle of student forms to her classroom. When I walked in everything was fine. It was quiet reading time in her classroom and I politely said excuse me for the interruption, and then placed the forms on the corner of her desk. Before I was able to turn around, she requested that I come back to the corner of her desk. "Are you a gang-member?" she asked staring at me intensely. I had never felt so uncomfortable. Completely thrown for a loop by the inquiry, I embarrassingly stated "no" and left her classroom to finish my errands. It wasn't until later that day, while talking to my friends Chris, Lewis, Eric, and Frank, that I truly discovered the implications of her question. Given my history with these particular teachers, I was very hurt to be told by them I couldn't join the school's reading club.

As tears began to form in the wells of my eyes, I looked at my former math teacher in disbelief. All she had to offer was a sly smirk, as she stared back; totally living out her infamous nickname of, "the Redheaded Witch of the North." I felt defeated and helpless. All I could do was exit the classroom dropping my head as I exited. I slowly made my way down the hall, grazing the steel lockers with my left shoulder, to join my friends for our daily normal walk home. Out of nowhere, I felt a tap on my right shoulder.

To my surprise it was Eric. "What's going on, Jay?"

"Nothing much… just thinking about how much I hate this school. What's up with you?" I replied.

"That's all?! I thought something bad happened. I hate this school too but that's nothing new." Eric expressed with a surprised look on his face, "Everything I like to do they don't have, and the things they have I don't like. I liked school when I was in kindergarten though."

"That's crazy," I remarked. "I felt like that too until this morning. Do you remember when Ms. Williams made that announcement about the school starting a reading club?"

"Yeah…"

"Well I went to sign up for it, and that evil teacher Ms. Rash and Ms. Jasper said that I didn't 'fit the description.' Can you believe that?" I asked while holding my hands out with the intention of receiving an argument.

And Eric didn't let me down, "Man I told you before…they don't like us! If I were you I'd tell my mother, because you know my moms wouldn't stand for that."

"Yeah I know, but I wouldn't want to worry her with this; besides, my parents have enough to worry about," I explained while lowering my head and cutting the conversation short. I knew the rest of our friends were probably waiting for us outside.

As we continued to walk, Frank, Lewis and Chris could be seen from a distance waiting for us, as expected, at our usual meeting area – at the steps of the school's main entrance. As we walked up, Eric brought them up to speed about my disappointing news.

"Personally, I think you should tell your parents," Frank said in agreement with Eric.

"Man, whatever!" Lewis chimed in, "It's not like it would change the situation anyway. Forget that reading....book....or whatever the club is called. Shoot, we can start our own club!"

We all turned and looked at each other in total surprise, "Are you serious?" The idea coming from Lewis was crazy enough. He continually expressed how boring he thought reading was. He'd rather be up and active, than idle for any period of time. Regardless of how flabbergasted we were by his sporadic statement, Lewis was on to something. But the big question was, "How would we form our own group?"

Frank was always eager to take first stab on new ideas. "So what should we call ourselves?," he exclaimed in excitement.

"Whatever it is, it better not be weak," Lewis remarked while attempting to stand with sturdy posture.

"He's always acting like he's hard. Man shut up." Chris declared looking to down play Lewis' regular tough guy routine.

"Come shut me up then!!!"

"The both of you need to be cool. You all are always trying to fight each other." I interceded, making an effort to keep the conversation on track. "I have an idea. What about "The Reader's Circle?"

"Yeah…That's it!," we shouted in unison. One obstacle down and now we were ready to continue the 'start-up' process. The next item up for discussion: where would we meet??? We all had suggestions, but in the end we agreed on a place in the woods not too far from where we lived. Everyone vowed a declaration of silence in regards to our self-established group. We didn't want anyone thinking we were sensitive. Looking back on it, and even now I realized that many of the boys we knew then strayed away from other kids because they felt like sensitivity meant weakness.

As we all went our separate ways, I'm sure we all had our own perspectives about the group. Personally, I was extremely excited and continued to formulate in my mind, and on paper, how I would like for the meetings run; I just hoped my friends were as excited as I was. Chris on the other hand, most likely could care less about "The Reader's Circle;" he mainly went along with us no matter what. Frank, being the most thoughtful of the group (which resulted in him being the butt of many jokes) probably thought about how much this venture would help us to bond. Eric perhaps had mixed feelings about the group and our newly found endeavor; I say this because it has always been a task trying to figure out his thoughts – an introvert at its finest. Lewis, being a secret fan of drama, although he would probably deny with every ounce of blood in his body, probably thought about how much this could possibly help him with the ladies.

I believe everyone knew, without a shadow of doubt, that reading has always been a passion of mine; mainly, because it provided a chance for me to experience new things through the experience of reading the stories of others and providing an escape from my own. Problems at school…a great fictional story of going to a far distant land did the job; parent's arguing…an imaginative tale about possessing super powers provided the cure; or just the common case of boredom…a book with multiple endings, or never ending conclusions, would always seem to do the trick.

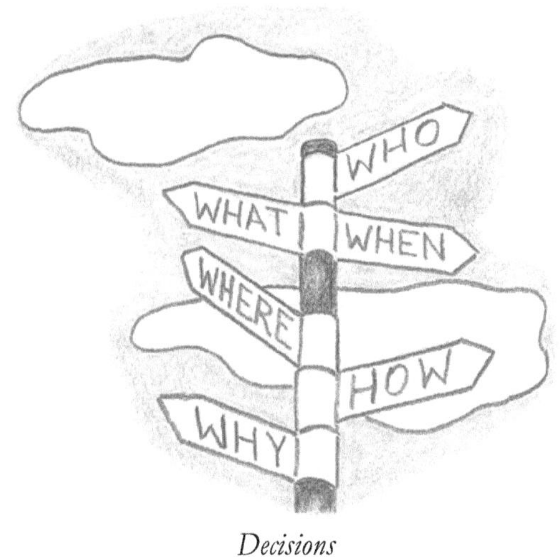

Decisions

2 ROUGH BEGINNINGS

The next morning we all woke up from our nights of slumber and went about our daily routines. As usual, I was abruptly awakened by my father as he rustled around the house. He worked as a secondary Social Studies and Math teacher at the local high school and was always the first to rise, waking me up. I rolled out of bed and followed the wonderful smell of breakfast which led me to a kiss from my mother. My mother worked as a seamstress. "Good morning baby," she greeted me as she planted a kiss on my forehead. We exchanged a few words as she packed up her patterns, material, and other supplies for work. After breakfast, and following my daily ritual of taking a vitamin C pill, and a well-known cartoon character-inspired multivitamin washed down by milk, I headed back to my room and got ready for school.

Frank's morning, on the other hand, was never that cut and dry. Frank would usually be awakened by the sound of his sisters getting ready for the day. Due to seniority, his two older sisters Sherry and Donna would help their mother get his two younger sisters April and Kimberly ready; so that meant his sisters had first dibs on the bathroom. When they were done, Frank would have his turn. His mother and sisters always had breakfast cooking for him by the time he was ready for school. After they all ate together at the kitchen table, Sherry and Donna headed off to work while

Frank, April, and Kimberly headed to school. Sherry worked downtown as a waitress for a well-known hotel named *Le Plaza*, while Donna served as the assistant director at *Toddler Academy* daycare. April and Kimberly were pre-school age, so Frank's mother would usually drop them off on her way to work. Frank's mother, Ms. Randle, ran her own restaurant until she hurt her back at the restaurant. As a result of her injury she eventually had to sell the restaurant and since then had been relying on insufficient disability coverage to provide for the family according to Frank. She also worked as the head of community relations at our families' church to make extra money for the children.

Lewis would usually be awakened by a yell from his father from the bottom of the stairway that echoed into his room, jolting him out of his sleep. After shaking off the night's sleep and the jolt, he would make his way downstairs to find an empty place with breakfast on the stove that his father would leave for him before darting off to work. Lewis's father was a butcher-by-day at *Meat and Chops* and a janitor-by-night at *Russell's Cleaning Services.* Lewis would normally eat his breakfast alone, and then head back up the stairs to finish getting ready for the school day.

Chris' morning, was drastically different from everyone's. He would wake up, most of the time, to his parents arguing; many times over money or whatever was troubling them at the time. His father would usually leave in a rage out of the back door to work. He worked at a marketing firm, *Neman, Dunn, and Brooks Marketing*; he started with two former teammates from his old days as a professional athlete. After his father's normal exit, his mother would then begin to prepare a breakfast for her and Chris while he got ready for school. Chris and his mother had a very close relationship. So much so, that his mother would usually lay out everything he needed for the day before she would head to work herself and start her duties of the secretary at the church.

Eric's morning(s) were like night and day in comparison to Chris'. His mother woke him up with a kiss on his cheek, followed by a "good morning" from his father. He would get ready for school and then head to the kitchen to eat breakfast with his mother, father, and younger sister, Angela, and talk about his day and other happenings. After breakfast, his father would begin his long day as an insurance agent for *Life Line Insurance* while his mother prepared her day as a stay at home mom. She enjoyed being at home with the kids and tending to their needs, but as they were growing up she hoped to get back into banking and accounting and made the decision to study for the CPA exam while being at home. Eric's family was super excited for his mother to be back in the work force doing what she enjoyed.

We call came from different backgrounds and family structures and had many differences as individuals, but one thing was for sure, nothing about our backgrounds, families, or differences could break our bond as brothers and friends.

Once I left my house, I would then meet Frank and Lewis at the same place every morning; by the fork in the road at the end of their neighborhood. Chris and Eric always rode to school with their mothers and on occasion Eric's father would take them. We would all meet together in the front hallway of the school before heading to our homeroom classes. Eric and I would see each other sporadically throughout the day, because of our similar class schedules. But Frank, Lewis and Chris saw each other the most because they were mostly in the same class all day. At lunch we were often escorted back to our respective lunch tables by the lunch monitor because we were unable to sit together but would try to find ways to talk to each other. But at the end of the day, all of that would change. When the last bell sounded for the day, we met at our designated meeting place and we would walk home together.

But the walk home on this particular day would be different. It would be the first official meeting for *The Reader's Circle.* As we made our way along the eight block walk toward our neighborhoods, we approached the wooded area that we designated as our official meeting place. Now to get to this place we had to go through a heavily-wooded area, travel over a small creek on a huge fallen oak tree that had been there long before any of us or even our parents-parents were ever thought of. After that, we would wiggle our way through a small open space to an area where at least a dozen oak trees circled a small parameter. This place was perfect for the group to meet. It was secluded and we were the only ones that knew about this secret spot as far as we knew.

"Here we are!" I shouted with such enthusiasm.

"Yeah…, yeah…," Lewis said indirectly.

Frank quickly jumped in asking, "Why are you always the one trying to wreck someone's mood?"

"Man, shut up and go turn some cartwheels or something." Lewis spatted back, operating in his normal ways.

"Someday somebody is gonna beat the breaks off of you," Frank shouted back in confidence, no doubt reciting something he heard from television.

"Whatever….even if it happens, I bet it won't be you!" Lewis claimed as he walked closer to Frank.

"You two chill out. One of you is always mad at the other. Are we going to go through with this, or will we have to stop before we start?" I said as my face backed up my obvious frustration.

"Nope, we're not stopping because of this. Let's just go on into the woods," Chris added with an exhausted look on his face.

"Yeah, let's just go." Eric commented.

So there we were, making our way through the thick of the woods coming to the big oak that bridged one side of the creek to the other - just a few more hops away from the small area that would become the official meeting spot for *The Reader's Circle.* As we stood looking at the vacant space as if it held the key to our destinies, the moment was suddenly cut short.

"Are you guys sure about this? I mean…us being out in the woods reading books and stuff. This just seems really feminine." Lewis stated.

"You say that about everything," Frank voiced.

"Whatever dude. What….did I offend you?" Lewis verbally gabbed back.

"Man I'll say this about the both of you….you two are acting like some little girls," said Chris, looking to intervene.

"Before all three of you get started as you usually do...if anyone wants to leave….be my guest," I replied annoyed.

"Bet! I'm out of here. I'll see you guys tomorrow at school," Lewis exclaimed and then walked off backtracking the way he came.

"I'm gone too," Frank retorted.

"Well looks like *The Reader's Circle* is over before it started, I'll see you at school tomorrow," Chris yelled as he trailed behind the two others.

"Well Jay, you ready to go too?" Eric asked.

"Man forget them, I'm not ready to leave. We don't need them to start this reading club anyway." I replied. "I know you brought those books in your bag for everyone, but since they ran out on us - you take a book and I'll take a book. Let's read some of it tonight, and then when we can come back tomorrow and discuss what we've read. Cool?"

"Alright, it's a plan," Eric replied. "I guess it's just me and you?"

"Yeah I guess so, but seriously did you think Lewis and Chris would be involved in a group that reads. The only way I thought they'd be involved was if some girls were going to be here, or if we were going to do something sports related." I remarked.

"I know, right," Eric answered shaking his head.

After Eric had unloaded his mother's collection of African-American literature, she collected during her time at college, the both of us selected the first two books on the top of the pile to read and left the official meeting place for *The Reader's Circle.* My pick was a classic by Richard Wright, *Black Boy.* I was excited to begin reading. The name alone was interesting seeing as to how it was something I could relate to as a young black boy. When I arrived home I rushed to finish my homework and ate dinner with my parents. After I successfully cleaned my plate, I ran to my room, pulled the book out of my backpack, got comfortable in a spot on the floor at the foot of my bed and dove into the new adventure. I was engulfed in the tale and before I knew it I had read nearly three-quarters of the book. I found myself intrigued with the main character. He reminded me a lot of myself. As I went to sleep I thought about my favorite part when the main character graduated from the ninth grade as valedictorian and gave his own speech rather than the speech everyone else said he should give to appease the crowd. The character's desire to be his own person were right up my alley, especially with what happened to me involving the reading club at school. As I closed my eyes to go to sleep I said aloud, "I will be like the boy in the book." While I might not have understood it all then, it was then that the seed was planted to be resilient in living out all of my dreams and goals no matter what anyone else said about me or whatever gets in my way.

Dismissal

3 THE FIRST MEETING

The next morning we all went through our daily routines to get to school. When I finally made my way to the fork in the road, I was overwhelmed with excitement. I had to let them know how much they missed out by not staying. Normally, the three of us would talk about a game we saw the night before, the ever so popular topic "girls", or what we were planning on doing that day but not on this particular day because I started the conversation.

"Man you all should've stayed yesterday. Eric and I had the meeting anyway after you two and Chris left us."

"Is that so? Ok, that's cool… So, I guess you guys just kicked us out of the group huh?" Lewis asked inquisitively.

"Whatever…we didn't kick any of you out. But we just want all of you to know that *The Reader's Circle* is going to take place if the three of you choose to be a part of it or not," I explained.

"I feel ya….well, I'll be there from now on," Frank stated.

"Yeah, me too," Lewis added. "What did you fellas talk about?"

"Eric had a few of his mother's books for us to choose from," I answered.

"WHAT?? He told his moms about *The Reader's Circle*?" Lewis exclaimed. "I thought we agreed that we wouldn't tell anybody about the group!"

"Relax! He didn't tell her about it…he always gets books from her to read," I answered calmly.

"I was about to say…," Frank said as if he was going to do something if he told.

"Well, anyways, I picked out this book titled *Black Boy.* I almost read the whole book last night, because it was tight. I'd tell you more, but I'll wait until tonight's meeting," I shared with excitement. "Are the two of you planning on joining us?"

"I'll be there," Frank expressed hoping to receive a mutual agreement.

"Yeah, I'll be there too," Lewis offered.

Frank, Lewis, and I finally made our way to school. As the school day proceeded, we all anticipated the upcoming meeting later that evening. When the bell rang at 3:00pm, we all met at our usual meeting spot and headed towards the woods. Once we arrived at the opening by the tree, we cut through the heavy brush and balanced ourselves across the big oak to finally reach our destination…the circle of big oaks.

"So how are we starting up the meeting today," Eric questioned?

"What are you talking about? You're talking crazy," Lewis replied.

"Look, there you go about to get yo….," Eric snapped back.

"Wow, wait a minute before the argument begins… You and Lewis need to chill before the same thing that happened yesterday, goes down," I intervened. "Now is this how you think we should run *The Reader's Circle*?"

"I think we should run *The Reader's Circle* like they used to run them roundtable meetings, voting on issues and stuff like that," Chris answered.

"Yeah, I think we should do that too," Frank agreed.

"So everybody's cool with that?," I asked.

Everyone all looked around at each other and answered in unison, "Yeah."

"So what do we do now, I never been to no book...reading….club," Frank asked.

"I guess since Eric and I were the only ones to read a book last night, we'll talk about what we've read so far. Then everybody'll give their comments," I offered. "How do you feel about that?"

The group members nodded in agreement.

"You wanna go first or do you want me to start?" I asked Eric.

"You can start," Eric replied.

"Bet... Well I read *Black Boy*, a book by this guy named Richard Wright. It had all kinds of crazy stuff in it. Lew, I think you'd really like this dude," I added to make sure I got his attention before he became uninterested.

"Why you say that?" Lewis asked with a furrowed brow.

"Because he was pulling out switch blades, stealing, doing whatever he had to do to get money…all of that," I explained.

"For real…..man I need to read that," Lewis replied.

I tried my best to hide the excitement I felt to see that he was so interested. "You can get it after I'm done; I have a few more chapters to read. But I think we should talk about what we would do if we were in his situation." I suggested.

"Yeah, that's cool. But we haven't read it," Chris added.

"I know that, but what I'm talking about is....say I read a book the night before our next meeting, then the next day I'll keep in mind some of the things I remembered about the book. Then we'll all have a chance to say what we would do in whatever the situation may be. You understand?" I explained.

"Oh....okay," Frank responded.

"Now in this book the main character gets beaten by his mother so bad that he almost dies, then his father left town with another woman. And on top of all that, he had to move with his mother out of town. So, what would you do if you were him?" I asked.

They all had an opportunity to voice their opinions, one by one. Of course the first one to express his view was Lewis. Lewis went on to tell everyone that he would've broke out and left everybody behind, especially if he had to fend for himself anyway. But he definitely shed light on how much he enjoyed hearing about the boy pulling knifes out on people. Chris explained that he would've tried to find his father and beat him down, because he said anyone that would just leave their family like that wasn't a man. Frank on the other hand, said that he would've just stayed with his mother and brother and if his father came back that he wouldn't even try to fight him. Eric shared that he would've stayed with his mother too, but wouldn't have resorted to drinking and getting into trouble because it would only add salt to the wound. When the conversation came back to me I was kind of torn between two choices: staying with my mother and picking up the slack of my father being removed, or leaving the whole situation and going out on my own. Deep down, I knew I would have probably stayed.

When we all decided that we had exhausted the discussion of *Black Boy*, we chose to move on to the book Eric read. The book was titled, *Invisible Man* by Ralph Ellison. Now if you've ever read this book you know how the story begins and if you're a young African-American male in the 21st century - *I feel your pain.* Of course, Eric explained to us that he didn't get passed the first chapter because it really bothered him that people would treat others like they did just to be evil. Of course, he had to follow his statement with an informative reason, because no one in our circle knew exactly what he was referring to. He began by trying to paint a picture of how the literature sketched a certain visual in his mind.

"Man, the main character was told if he got in front of a group of these white guys and gave a speech that he would get a scholarship, but they tricked him and had him fighting other black guys blind-folded for the scholarship," Eric implied.

"What!? Yeah right?" Lewis quickly replied.

"I'm serious….and they also had him running across an electric rug," Eric added.

"Stop lying," Frank insisted.

"I'm not bro, they were trying to humiliate him as much as possible. I guess to see if he really wanted the scholarship," Eric offered.

"Naw, they did it because they are evil people and they think that they own the world. Or they just wanted to treat him the same way they thought of him," Lewis inserted.

"Or it could be that they didn't want him to think he was advancing too much by getting a chance to go to college." Chris added.

"That's crazy. So did he go to college or what?", I asked.

"I don't know I'll have to tell you tomorrow, because after I read everything he went through. I needed to put it down for the night," Eric explained.

"Ok…" the whole group said to express the frustration we had for having to wait another night for the conclusion.

"Yeah you have to let us know, because if he's anything like old dude in *Black Boy* he's about to pull a blade out or something," Lewis stated intending to make a joke.

When our discussion over the *Invisible Man* began to come to an end we switched the flow of the meeting. Since I was almost done with my book and Eric had just scratched the surface of his, Chris, Lewis and Frank had to make their selections. After reading the back covers of the books; Frank chose James Baldwin's *Go Tell It on the Mountain* since he was into spiritual books and readings. Chris ravaged through the several remaining books, and decided on, *Fences* by August Wilson. Next it was Lewis' turn to choose. Unsurprisingly, he picked up the short pile of books and started the process of dropping one book to the ground after another hoping to find one that would spark his interest. He finally stopped at another Richard Wright piece, *Native Son.* I believe in part because of the impact *Black Boy* had on him.

After the three of them made their selections, we exited the woods and made our way to the street that would take us to our homes. Along the way, we talked about everything from television shows to the girls we joked about dating, just shooting the breeze, until the small group was down to one, me. After I entered my parent's home, and said hello to my mother, I headed straight to my room. As I dropped my backpack on the bed, I turned back to go downstairs to get something to drink. By then my father arrived back from the store and asked how my day went.

"It was just a regular day," I responded.

As I entered the kitchen, I revisited the wonderful smell I encountered as I walked into the house upon arriving home.

"Hey mom."

"Hey there, how was your day? Learn anything interesting at school?" My mother responded.

"No, just the regular....reading, writing, and arithmetic as they say," I said jokingly.

"Um Hmm, although I know you're being funny. I tell you all the time...'make sure you get a lesson out of your experiences. No matter what it is, because everything we go through, or experience in this life has a purpose."

"Yes ma'am, I know," I retorted.

While finishing my dinner, over a conversation with my mother and father, I began to think about the book I was reading and about how it would be if I was the main character. The thought alone made me appreciate being able to talk my parents and I would often share that much more. After finishing my meal, I kissed my mother and father goodnight, thankful for the ability and opportunities they provided to be able to talk to them and then headed to my room to finish my homework and get back to my book for *The Reader's Circle.* Once I completed my work and placed it in my backpack, I opened *Black Boy* and removed the bookmark from where I placed it the night before. After a couple hours, I began the final sentence of the book. Amazed and not let down by the way the book ended, I couldn't wait to let everyone know how it concluded. I was sure the other group members read bits and pieces of their book, but most likely not in comparison to my efforts.

Lewis Porter vs. Frank Neely

4 REPETITIVE ISSUES

The next morning Lewis, Frank, and I met at our usual meeting place to head to school. Frank and I seemed to be the only two excited about what we had read the night prior; Lewis, on the other hand, I'm sure didn't read a single word from the book and was in all probability planning on at least reading the table of contents before the end of the school day. On arrival, we went through our regular day, and I couldn't help but be distracted by the characters I read about in the book *Black Boy*. It seemed like every teacher I saw throughout the day reminded me of one of the characters in the book. Meanwhile, my friends seemed to go about their day as usual. Out of the other four, I would guess Eric and Frank were the only two that actually read anything the night before. Chris and Lewis I could almost guarantee were really only going through the motions, because they didn't want to feel left out. As the day slowly came to a close, the likelihood of Chris and Lewis scanning through the table of contents was high; especially, before their secret of being totally oblivious to what their selections were about. "Ding…Ding"…. Three o'clock finally hit and we began to assemble at our normal meeting location. Down the road we went; awaiting the navigational marker to our official meeting point for our newly founded group "*The Reader's Circle*." When we arrived at the big circle of oak trees, we took our seats and started the meeting.

Eric started the meeting with a question, "So what did everyone think about their books?"

Chris and Lewis commenced to looking around, clearly giving themselves away. As I looked at my counterparts, I secretly waited for at least one of my friends to speak up and illustrate just a hint of the enthusiasm I had bottled inside. But before I could speak out Frank timidly asked,

"Do you all want to hear about the book I read? I know you guys don't get into the spiritual stuff like I do."

"You straight… Go ahead and tell us about your book." I answered.

Frank said solemnly, "Good…., because I really enjoyed this book. The book I chose is called *Go Tell It on the Mountain.* It's by James Baldwin and it's a story about a fourteen year old kid named John, and John talks from his parent's perspective on issues of their lives. He tries to connect the thoughts and accounts back to his grandmother who was a slave in the south and what he has experienced in his neighborhood and life."

Eric stated, "Oh….I remember that book. My mother read it to me before when I was younger."

"Awe…isn't that sweet. His mother used to read to him," Lewis said making a face.

Frank suddenly lashed out, "See there you go again….you always trying to start something with somebody. One day somebody's going to beat you down, and I hope I'm there to see it."

"If somebody does, I guarantee it won't be you who does it," Lewis said in rebuttal.

I felt compelled to offer to a peaceful solution once again, "Alright…, alright…, everyone needs to chill out. It's a broken record with you two. Both of you need to calm down!"

Frank claimed, "I'm fine, it's just Lewis being Lewis. He's doesn't know when to stop and shut up."

Lewis spouted back, "Whatever man, you just soft. If I accidentally sneezed too hard you would probably be offended."

Frank retaliated as he stood to his feet, "I'll show you soft, I'm tired of this! What you wanna do?"

Lewis laughed, "You better sit down before I get up and smack the taste out cha mouth."

"Try it!," Frank yelled.

Lewis slowly stood to his feet worry-free, and muttered "You thin…." Then jumped toward Frank and pushed him to the ground. The rest of us immediately hopped to our feet and broke up the fight between Frank and Lewis.

"That's what will happen to you every time you talk to me like that," Lewis sparked off.

Frank stood in silence with a look of extreme inner-pain, as if he just swallowed a handful of nails.

"Man, you have to leave. This is your second time doing this…and you know we're trying to get this thing started. No more…if that's your intention just go ahead and head home and stay there!," I yelled in Lewis's direction.

"So you're taking Frank's side?" Lewis asked looking into my eyes.

"I'm not taking anyone's side! It's Frank's turn to speak, so he's not leaving. If it would've been your turn, you'd stay and he'd leave. That is if you ever decide to read anything in the first place."

Lewis intently made eye contact with all the others and simply said, "I don't wannabe part of this club 'thang' anyway, y'all can keep it!"

Everybody looked at Lewis with a look that echoed 'there he goes again.' As he walked away, the rest of us started to take our sits one after the other until no one was left standing.

"So Frank, are you ready to tell us what the book is about?," I asked trying to get things back on track.

"Naw, not tonight. I really don't feel up to it anymore. I'll do it next time."

"Come on Frank…don't let Lewis ruin another meeting," Chris offered.

"Like I said…not tonight. I mean, the night doesn't have to stop because I don't feel like talking about my book. We can talk about something else."

"Ok, something else like what? I would suggest Chris to take your turn but we all know he didn't read anything," I said putting Chris on the spot.

"What? How do you know if I read or didn't read anything?"

"Come on Chris…everyone sitting around this circle knows you haven't read one page out that book. Heck, Lewis even knows it and he's not even here," Eric added.

While trying to hold in a huge guilty laugh, Chris admitted, "ok, maybe I didn't read a page of the actual book yet…but at least I scanned the table of contents."

"That's a complete shame… Not only did you not read a single page of the book, but you couldn't even find it in yourself to read the table of contents," I said piggy-backing off of both statements.

And the only response Chris could come up with was, "hahaha…you ain't right."

We continued to go back and forth with Chris for a little while longer until the conversation moved on to what superhero we would be if we had super powers and what type of superhero powers we would like to possess. Our conversations of fancy ensued until the beginnings of night started to overcome the dawn of the day.

Chris Dunn

5 BITTER BLOOD

During the second meeting, the first real meeting, of our own self-assembled reading club officially known as the *The Reader's Circle*, we decided not to meet on the weekends, instead we would meet at a local park to play basketball or ride bikes around the neighborhood. On some occasions we would visit each other's houses to play video games. On this particular Saturday we chose to head to the park and play a game of twenty-one. The game of twenty-one on the courts is a basketball game with an objective of trying to be the first player to score twenty-one points; and if you so happen to be the first player to reach this score - you win the game. In addition, one of the rules in this game is if a player can catch the basketball after another player misses the shot and the ball bounces off the rim and takes a shot mid-air and makes it – that player takes away points from the competitor that initially missed the shot. There was no such thing as a foul. It was like a game of rugby but only with a basketball and no timeouts. We all really enjoyed this game except for Eric, because he was shorter and a little chubbier than the rest of us. Nevertheless, he played anyway. Chris was the roughest participant of us all, Lewis wouldn't agree. Lewis thought he was the best point-guard in the world; when he had the ball he would dribble it full-force with his head down to the basket, and when he was a defender – he would mercilessly hack anyone who had possession of the ball that came toward the basket. Frank mostly stayed on the outside perimeter when he attempted to score and had a really good jump shot. Myself, well I was said to be the best well-rounded player of the group, I wasn't known to be exceptionally great in any particular area, but I guess I was above average in every aspect of the game in my opinion.

As Chris held the ball in our third game of twenty-one and was looking to score the last two remaining points necessary for him to win, six kids from a neighborhood on the other side of town just happened to be passing by. Within the group of kids there was Shawn Poser, Joe Nathan, Marcus Schrader, Ray Ford, Crawford Bennett, and Al Jones. Joe, Shawn, Al, and Ray were on bikes while Marcus and Crawford were riding on their handlebars. As they approached the courts, Shawn yelled out,

"How about a game???"

And Lewis, being known to welcome any challenge responded, "Bring it!!! Five against five though!"

Since the other group had more than the agreed number, they decided to flip a coin. After all the winner's coins had landed face up, they approached the court with determination in every step.

"You all want to shoot for first ball?," Crawford asked.

"Nope, since you're visiting…you can shoot first. But if you miss…it's our ball," Lewis responded quickly.

Ray replied, "Wait a minute, it's supposed to be whoever makes it takes it!"

"I know! But we don't miss when we shoot."

"Is that so?"

Lewis slyly answered, "Yeah, that's so!"

Now to explain the history of these two won't take a long time. Lewis and Ray used to be best friends, and now it seemed as if they were each other's worst enemy. They haven't been very fond of each other since Ray moved to the other side of town. Ray's family used to be next door neighbors with Lewis and his father before he moved, but that wasn't the real reason behind them becoming so bitterly-cold toward one another. Their rivalry actually started from an incident that occurred early last summer at the town's local fair. Lewis was with his cousin, Darius (better known as 'Duke') and saw Ray standing in line waiting to ride one of the rides. So Lewis went over to say hello and was caught off guard by Lewis's response. Lewis greeted Ray with a "what's up," but didn't get a response in return. In disbelief, Lewis said "what's up" once more and still got no response. Instead, all Lewis received was an empty expression. Lewis in turn called him a punk; followed by a few other statements of disapproval and went as far to push him. Of course, that's when Ray said something back and offered a push as well. The pushing escalated into fighting until Lewis' cousin and other spectators separated the two of them. As a result of the altercation there was now bitter blood between the old friends. This was the first time Lewis and Ray had seen each other since the fair, which made the tension on the basketball court very thick.

"Cool…make it take it then," I interjected in an effort to eliminate any further tension.

"What?!" You mean to tell me that you're backing down from this coward?" Lewis questioned.

"Who you calling coward…little man?" Ray responded.

Those words ignited Lewis. If there was anything that pushed his buttons it was being called "little." There was actually a tale of what Lewis did the last time someone called him "little" or "small." Lewis' cousin Duke called him "small" once and he hit him in the head with a video gaming console. Ray knew this statement bothered Lewis, thus adding fuel to the fire.

"WHAT DID YOU JUST CALL ME?!!" Lewis shouted taking a step forward.

"Whoa…whoa, we're not going there. Just forget about it…he didn't say anything." I insisted.

Lewis didn't buy it at all, but didn't say anything else. He just tilted his head up and stared at Ray. We all elected Frank to shoot for us, while our opposition chose Shawn. Shawn shot first……BRICK! Now it was Frank's turn to shoot… SWISH!!! It was our ball!

As everyone made their choices of who to guard, or check, Chris stepped in front of Lewis, "I got Ray…and Lewis…you take Crawford."

Lewis reluctantly went along with it.

As Eric stood out of bounds, I freed myself from my defender and received the inbound pass from Eric. While I was making my way to the top of the arc, I spotted Chris driving down the middle and dished a no look pass to setup him up for the easy bucket. A little under a minute into the game the score was already 2-0, and we were up. Our confidence was sky-high, and Lewis definitely expressed his vocally. This sparked a chain reaction amongst the defense because they weren't about to give up that easy. Once again, Eric took the ball out and in bounced a pass to me. This time around I decided to take a little more time with the ball so I could really see how the other team was guarding us. That was until I noticed Shawn giving Frank too much distance and fed him a quick pass behind the three-point line. Although Frank made "the make-it-take-it" shot, the other team didn't know how good of a shooter he really was and it was nothing but net! As a team, we scored four more consecutive baskets until the ball was rebounded over Eric by Al. The rest of the game was really intense; a few words here and there and an occasional hard foul or two, but of course those were never called because no one wanted to be looked at as weak by the opposing team.

And there we were - in possession of the ball and looking to potentially score the last two points of the game. We were up 19-14 and Eric was taking the ball out. Since I was normally the "go-to" guy, I was being double-teamed while the rest of the team was running around to free them of the full-court press. Then all of a sudden Chris lost Ray and Eric threw him the ball. After taking a few dribbles he unloaded a nice in-between the legs pass to Lewis. Lewis catching the pass on the run took the ball strongly down the middle and was hammered to the ground by Crawford along with the assistance of Ray; but not before Lewis was able to put up a shot. Before the ball finished bouncing around the rim and eventually going in the basket, Lewis looked up to see the culprits who knocked him down. It didn't matter who was involved because as soon as he discovered Ray had a hand in it - his temper exploded! Lewis quickly jumped to his feet from the ground as if his bottom was on fire, cocked back and let off a barrage of punches landing about 85% of them. Lewis' reaction to the hard foul sparked an all-out brawl. The altercation lasted long enough to catch the attention of a policeman driving by the park.

"RUN!!!" yelled Eric.

Everyone immediately dispersed and we ran in one direction and the crew from the other side of town ran in the other. We were all scared of getting caught and having our parents find out what just happened. In any other instance, Lewis would have run toward the police, because he thought they were the coolest. They saved people, were able to walk around everywhere with a gun, could drive as fast as they wanted to, and they seemed to be respected by everyone. This occasion however was vastly different.

After running, for what seemed to be forever, I yelled to everyone else:

"I think we lost them…"

"I think we did too." Chris replied.

"I don't know about anybody else, but I'm about to die of thirst!" Eric exclaimed.

"What about Gimpy's? I could really go for one their hamburgers right about now too!"

"With what…? I know I don't have any money." Lewis confessed.

"Don't worry about it. I got you." Frank answered.

"Ok cool!"

The relationship between Frank and Lewis was a funny one. They always seem to be in constant conflict with each other, but every once in a while we would witness a moment such as this. A couple of years back, when Frank was being bullied by a group of upperclassmen, Lewis came along and risked being jumped by not only bigger kids…but a large number of them on Frank's behalf.

Once we caught our breath after all the commotion at the park, and running away afterwards, we were on our way to Gimpy's. Gimpy's was a local burger and shake joint located not too far from our area of town. Although it was located in a busier part of town, close to a popular gas station that was down the same street on the corner and across the street from a shopping plaza, it never really got much service. We visited Gimpy's regularly though and they had the best burgers in town in our opinion. After placing and receiving our usual orders, we all decided to go against our rule of not meeting on the weekends and headed towards the woods.

Along the way everyone shared their own versions of how the altercation took place with Crawford and his friends from the other side of town, but the fact remained - we knew in the back of our minds that we would probably run into them again. There were only five of us against the six we played against, plus the countless others they were related to. Despite the facts we would all concur that although we didn't have any brothers, or a huge number of family members in town, we would be ok. We considered ourselves more than friends, we were brothers.

Frank Neely

6 A BROTHERLY BOND

After a few playful shoves and friendly banter as we crossed the big oak to our designated meeting place, we all took our usual positions. Since it was getting a little late, I decided to put some of my Boy Scout talents to use by lighting a fire. I liked to sit on this one particular tree that seemed to have grown specifically to fit my shape, so there I sat. Lewis being the more rebellious member of the group always wanted to climb one of the trees and make his seat wherever he seemed to fit in the treetop. Chris always liked looking at the stars, so he chose to lie down on his back and rest his head on one of the big roots growing out of one particular tree. Eric and Frank both set Indian-style and used their personally selected trees to support their backs.

When our meeting officially began, we decided to begin by asking who wanted to talk about the book they chose. Before anyone had the chance to say anything Lewis interrupted by saying, "I suggest that since I messed up the last meeting when Frank was about to tell us about his book, I think he should have first dib's." We were all taken aback by these words. Our mouths open and jaws dropped. In an unconscious synchronized effort we all responded. "Ok….."

Frank was always the most animated in the group. It wasn't surprising that he couldn't stay seated to tell us about his book. He stood up and took his place in the middle of the circle. Although Frank didn't have the book with him, he stood as if he had it memorized. We were rather discombobulated by his actions, but this was Frank's personality.

Frank started to speak, "The book I read….," followed by a long pause.

"Well get it out why don't cha!" Lewis spouted out.

"Take it easy on him Lewis… Frank it's ok, just take your time." I calmly suggested hoping to ease Frank's hesitation.

"It's ok Frank…get it off your chest," Chris affirmed looking at Lewis with a look that implied silence on Lewis' part.

"Yeah come on Frank, don't keep us waiting," Eric stated to add his support.

After Frank took a swallow and had a long deep breath, he began his interpretation of the book. "I really identified with this book because I really connected with the main character, John. I don't know if you all knew this or not, but I've never met my biological father and my sisters and I have different fathers. I have always wondered, in secret, who my father was, or is, and why I'm the only sibling of my family to have a different father than my sisters. While I was reading this book, I started to feel like I have developed a certain level of hatred for my real father. Sometimes I feel like I was a mistake or what I have heard older people call an illegitimate child. I never told anyone how I felt until now, so please don't repeat this to anyone."

"I never would have guessed any of that, but I'm glad you shared this secret with us and you have my word that I will never repeat any of your words to anyone outside of this circle," I said with empathy breaking the awkward silence.

"You have my word too!" Eric added.

"Your secret is safe with me too, Frank," Chris chimed in.

Then suddenly Lewis climbed down from his seat in the tree and stood on the ground facing the middle of the circle for a moment, then proceeded to walk toward Frank. Once Lewis made his way within a few feet of Frank, close enough for him to see the tears in his eyes, Lewis reached out to Frank with both arms and hugged him. The group sat in a silent shock.

"Don't worry…everything will be alright," Lewis said comforting Frank, then he turned around and walked toward the direction of the big oak.

"Where are you going?" I asked confused.

"I forgot that I had to finish something for my father before he gets home," answered Lewis.

We all knew that Lewis wasn't telling us the whole truth, but we accepted it for what it was worth. Being that our meeting was rather emotional, we decided to close out the meeting earlier than usual. We extinguished the fire, and headed back to our homes. Traveling back through the woods, and eventually entered into our neighborhoods, I couldn't help but notice how melancholy the night seemed. While briefly reflecting over the evening's events and the bond we had as friends, I had an epiphany. When one of us is impacted in a certain way, the four of us seemed to be impacted the same. We were truly brothers at heart, and the fact that Lewis and Frank were obviously bothered by the underlying premise of the book Frank shared at the meeting, we were all bothered. As we shouted our "see-ya-laters," we subconsciously agreed without saying that everything would be alright with time.

As the night's stars began to disappear and the sun peaked above the trees on the outskirts of town, and the days from Sunday to Monday leaped from one to the next, I found myself looking at Lewis and Frank waiting for me in the distance at our usual meeting place.

"What took you so long? Frank and I have been waiting for you for about…(*glancing at his watch*) for about 15 to 20 minutes." Lewis expressed.

Although he was right all I could mutter back was, "Whatever. As if you've never been late before."

"Ha! Ha Ha! Funny man. Although you may be right, you know it's always cold out here in the mornings," he retorted sarcastically.

"Yeah, yeah. I know. It can be rather brisk at times."

As we laughed at my attempt to use terms outside of our normal vernacular, I couldn't help but notice something was holding back the usual intensity of Lewis' laughter.

"Hey Lew.. Are you ok? For some reason you don't seem like yourself this morning. What's up?" I asked.

"Aw man, I'm good. I just have a lot on mind. That's all."

"Well, you know we're here for you if you ever need to talk about anything?" Frank added.

"Yeah, I know. Thanks, but I'm good though," Lewis assured with a look that suggested otherwise.

"Ok but if you ever need to, just let us know," I reaffirmed.

"Aight, appreciate it," Lewis responded. Lewis didn't do a very good job at concealing his emotions. He looked as though he wanted to say something but couldn't.

Although I wanted Lewis to accept my invitation to talk, I dropped it and reassured myself that he would open up when he was ready. I decided not to push him and joined the conversation. The topic of discussion today was, who were the finest girls in school and Lewis' ridiculous accusations about not paying them any attention because he was only interested in girls in middle school and high school. After listening to a few handfuls of Lewis' empty promises, we finally arrived to our destination, Piedmont Elementary.

Although it was a Friday and I was overjoyed by the fact that I wouldn't have to sit through another day of this school's boredom and frequent brain-farts caused by my lack of interest in my classes, I was more excited about meeting with the fellas later so we could continue our literary discussions. With every minute seeming to pass slower than the prior, I could clearly see that Ms. Wheeler's clock didn't share my same enthusiasms. But as the hands on the clock finally made their way to the 10 second countdown, I positioned my feet as if I was an unnumbered Apollo space shuttle. T minus…3, 2, 1…and I was off. Before I met up with the guys I had to make a quick stop at my locker. After aligning the final number on the combination lock, I heard the voice of Dalm.

"What's up Jay?" Dalm asked.

"Just grabbing this book I need for Ms. Cameron's class. You know we have her yearly science project coming up in a couple of weeks, so I'm trying to get a head start."

"Oh, ok. Well I guess I know who I'll be asking for help?!" He casually proposed.

(Both of us laughed at the fact he was joking and serious at the same time.)

"Ok, I gotcha covered."

"Good looking out Jay! Ay, you going to Allison's skate party tonight?"

"Tonight? Umm, I'm not sure because I totally forgot about it. Are you?"

"Heck yeah! I'm surprised you forgot about it?! Everybody has been talking about it all week." He responded with utter excitement.

"Ok cool. Well, I may be there…hopefully my parents won't mind," I stated.

"I feel ya. Well, hopefully you'll be able to go because it's going to be packed!"

"Yeah, me too. Ok, I'll holla at ya later."

"Cool. Peace out!" Dalm yelled out while seemingly running to his next destination.

After I got everything I needed from my locker, I headed toward the school's entrance to meet up with the crew. As one of the front doors swung open, I could see the top of Chris' head bobbing above the top step from my view outside. With every step that brought me closer, I could begin to see the remaining "club" members. Before I could get a word out...

"Dang…you're late again! First, you had me and Frank standing in the cold waiting on you this morning. Now, you have all of us waiting after school. What's the deal?" sparked Lewis.

"Oh, whatever… you've probably been waiting for like half a second," I snapped back. "Anyways, I was late because I was talking to Dalm and he was telling me about Allison's skating party tonight. Do you all want go because he said it's supposed to be packed?"

(A brief commotion erupted amongst us with approval with the exception of Frank.)

"Well, what about the meeting?" Frank asked quietly.

"I know, I thought about that too before I brought up the skating party," I stated to offset the confusion I felt brewing.

"Man, we can postpone our meeting until tomorrow. I mean, do you realize how many girls will be there?" Lewis stated excitedly.

"Wait a minute… I thought you said you weren't interested in the girls our age? James, don't you remember him saying that earlier?" Frank said with a smirk.

"Yeah, Frank is right… You did say that," I agreed.

"I know what I said…and I meant it! What I'm saying right now is that I know Allison's older sister will be with some of her friends, and I'll be trying to see what's up with them," Lewis said simply responded trying to save face.

"….whatever! We know the truth. But it's all good," Chris exclaimed trumping Lewis' bogus excuse.

"Hahaha, right! I hate to break up this comedy session, but how are we going to get there? I know my father won't be able take us tonight, so I would have to ask my mom. What about your parents?" I asked the group.

"No good on my end, you know my situation," answered Lewis.

"Right, it's a wrap with me too," Chris followed.

"Both of my older sisters have to work tonight, and my mother will be home with the other two. So, I'm not an option." shared Frank.

"I'm sure my mother could take us, but your mother would probably have to pick us up though," Eric offered.

"Ok, I'll check when I get home and give everyone a call," I responded feeling myself getting more excited.

"Cool," the group said in unison as we went our separate ways.

Rollers

7 A HEART'S PARDON

When I finally made it home I saw my mother carrying some fabrics and other materials through the garage. So I ran over to offer her some help.

"Hey mom! Do you need any help?"

"Oh, hey baby! Sure, grab that box in the back seat and close the garage for me," she replied giving me a kiss on the cheek.

"Ok, I got it," I said running to the car to retrieve the supplies.

I hurried to grab the box from the back seat. As I walked toward the house I thought about how I would ask my mother to take us to the party. I knew I had to keep my cool. She was always particular about me going places and wanted to know the specifics about everything. Will there be adults there? What kids will be there? What time things started and ended? I learned that I needed to be able to answer all the questions before I asked. I found my mother in the family-room putting away the materials and fabrics from her store.

"Go ahead and put that box down by the door," she instructed, "how was your day?"

"It was fine, but I'm glad it's Friday and I don't have to go to school tomorrow," preparing to build my case for the party.

"I hear ya," she laughed. "Well, I see you are home early. I'm surprised you aren't out playing with your friends."

"Uh oh…" I thought. I wasn't exactly ready to ask her about the skating party at that moment, but I decided to fight against my apprehensions. "Well…we were..but…" I found myself stumbling over my words trying to find the courage to ask if she could give us a ride.

"But what? Is everything ok?," she asked with concern.

"Yes mama…everything is ok," I assured her.

"Well? What is it?," she asked growing more concerned by the moment.

"Well…a girl at our school is having a skating party tonight, and I would like to go…can I?," I asked relieved that I had finally gotten it out.

"Does this girl have a name?"

"And here come the questions," I thought, "Yes, her name is Allison."

"Ok... Allison who?"

"Allison Davis"

"Davis…? Davis…? Oh, Gloria's daughter?," she asked.

"Yes ma'am," I answered anxiously.

"Well, you know my concerns - will her parents be there, what time does it start, and when is it over, etcetera?," she added.

"I believe her parents will be there…I can check though," I exclaimed before she shut me down completely, "I think it starts at 6 and it'll probably be over at around 8 or 9?"

"Well until you can give me some specific details, the jury is still out." she replied.

"Yes ma'am." I felt relieved and happy that she didn't totally excuse the idea.

I immediately called Eric to find out what his mother said about the party and her driving us to it. After a few three-way calls, I was on the phone with the whole crew.

"Eric, can you mother take us?," I asked anxiously.

"Yep," Eric responded excitedly.

"Cool. Do you know if her parents will be there?," I asked hoping he would be able give the information I needed to give my mother.

"Her parents will be there. It starts at 5 and ends at 8," Eric reported.

"Thanks man! Everyone else ready for tonight?," I asked in excitement.

"Man I'm just ready to see some fine older girls," Lewis responded.

"Man this is going to be fun! I'm going to go pick out my clothes right now," Frank exclaimed.

"I guess," Eric said quietly.

"It's going to good. Ok fellas. I'll see you all in a bit," I said trying to mask my excitement. It was going to the party of the school year.

Destination: "Rollers" Skating Rink
Day & Time: Friday, 5-8pm

Transportation: Drop-off/Eric's mother (Mrs. Thomas), Pick-up/my mother (Mrs. Waters)
Chaperons: Allison's parents and the parents of Allison's close friends
My Mother's Decision: Yes!!!

I sat on the edge of my bed gazing out of my window waiting for Mrs. Thomas to arrive. I would be able to see her pull up into our driveway from my bedroom window. I would be picked up last because my house was on the way to the skating rink. I glanced at the hands of the clock on my wall approaching 4:40. With each tick I felt myself becoming more anxious. After falsely identifying at least a dozen car lights coming down the road, I finally recognized Eric's mother's car slowly approaching my parent's sidewalk. Only stopping to grab a few belongings on my way to the door, I ran into the kitchen and alerted my mother of Mrs. Thomas' arrival and to confirm the meeting place where she would pick us up after the skating party.

Although I was eager to get to the car to meet my friends, I had to keep my cool and in turn tried to maintain a slow stroll to the car. By the time I reached the sidewalk I could no longer keep my composure and my stroll turned into a slow jog the rest of the way. When I got into the car I greeted my friends and thanked Mrs. Thomas for driving us to the party. On the way to the party the conversation was minimal and cordial, but once we arrived and exited the vehicle we were our usual selves. After Mrs. Thomas let us out, we knew we had to be on our best behavior because she would be watching us until we went into the skating rink. As we walked up to the entrance, I couldn't help but look around at the crew. I'm pretty sure to everyone else we were walking at normal pace; but to us, it felt like we were walking in slow motion to theme music in one of those Blaxploitation movies in my parent's movie collection. Our brief moment of fame would soon be cut short when we realized Mrs. Thomas didn't drive off like we thought. She was now speaking with Allison's parents at the front door. I felt embarrassment come over me. We looked at each other with the feeling that our perfectly well orchestrated plan had gone wrong. Once we were able to pick our pride up from the ground, we made our way into the skating rink and started to socialize with our fellow classmates. We made a few short rounds through the crowd as we made our way the counter to exchange our sneakers for roller-skates. Once we collected our skates, we made our way to the rink and joined with the rotation.

Now, I wasn't the best of skaters on regular skates, but I knew how to handle a pair of roller blade. I would have put on a show for the whole crowd. Tonight the old school four wheel skates would have to do. I tried my best to blend in with the crowd and mask my lack of confidence. The rest of the crew, I must admit was comedy. Out of the crew as a whole,

Frank, was the best skater by far. He was never shy around the ladies, and somehow found a way to draw a large number of girls around him to dance along with. Lewis, tried to keep up with Frank the best he could but Lewis was nowhere near as good a skater and consequently slid all over the rink. I had to give it to him though, he didn't show any fear or reservation. Chris always seemed to be good at any and everything athletic, so he took to skating extremely fast around the ring. Eric on the other hand was more insecure about his skating ability and stayed on the outer parameter of the rink.

So there we were, without a doubt, making our presence known at the party, or so we thought. No one could tell us anything different. None of that really mattered to me though. There was one person at the party I particularly wanted to grab the attention of, but I was failing miserably. Her name was Melanie Evans, and I had a crush on her since the second grade. She was the type of girl you could tell all the guys wanted at least in my opinion. *I know what you're thinking…how come I never approached her, right?* Well, it seemed to me that Melanie was into older guys and I honestly assumed I never had a chance. That didn't mean I couldn't admire her from a distance. As I was admiring I saw Olivia Summers approaching me. Olivia and I had been in the same classes since kindergarten and she could be so annoying at times, but I would try to be as nice as I could until I couldn't take it anymore. I would often have to find a way to escape to safety.

"Hey James, I didn't know you were going to be here." Olivia said trying to strike up a conversation. I immediately started to feel trapped.

"Yeah, I forgot all about it until this morning. But the crew and I decided to come at the last minute," I responded looking around trying to find something, someone, ANYTHING to be my scapegoat.

"You're right…a lot of people didn't know about it because Allison didn't want the whole school to be here, only a select 'few'," she explained.

"I hear ya but it looks like a lot people didn't get that memo, because it is packed in here," I pointed out.

"This is true. I don't know about anyone else, but I'm glad that memo didn't go for you," she stated with a funny look in her eyes. It was getting awkward.

"Uh,….thanks?? I'm glad it didn't either," I replied returning a puzzled look as a result of my confusion. I had to find something to get me out of this conversation. Finally, it came to me...the restroom! She couldn't follow me there. "Well, Olivia I'll catch up with you a little later. I gotta run to the restroom before the limbo starts."

"Ok James, that's fine…I'll be waiting for you."

Walking away from Olivia I couldn't help but wonder what was going on with her. She was acting so strange. The inquiry held my attention briefly before I noticed Melanie was looking at me while I walked toward the restrooms. "Surely I was just imagining that…I know she didn't just look at me," I thought. The entire time I was in the restroom, I replayed the image of her looking at me in my mind. After managing to convince myself I was only imagining things, I walked out of the restroom only to find Melanie standing exactly where I was talking to Olivia. In any other circumstance I would have avoided walking in her direction, or just passed by her without making eye contact. This time was different because she was standing by the crew and I didn't see a way of escaping the situation. I took a deep breath and began my confident walk of nervousness. As I approached Melanie, she turned her head in my direction and caught my eye. It was as if time stood still and all noise ceased. Her smile left me paralyzed. I must have been standing there for a moment. I was pulled from my trance when I heard someone speaking. Little did I know it was Melanie.

"Sorry. What did you say?," I asked with embarrassment.

"I said…are you enjoying the party?," she asked softly.

"Oh…ok. Yeah, so far I am. I'm with my guys…we usually have fun everywhere we go." I expressed trying to play it cool and hide my shock that I was actually having a conversation with Melanie Evans.

"So you're only here with your guys? And…you didn't come here to meet up with Olivia?"

"Olivia?" I said bewildered. "Are you serious? Naw, you got it all wrong…I didn't know she was gonna be here. She's like…an annoying distant cousin," I said repulsively. The last thing I needed was anyone thinking I liked Olivia.

"Oh yeah? Well it just seemed like that is what was going on. Or at least to someone interested, that may have wanted to know," Melanie expressed with a look similar to the one Olivia tried to give earlier, only it was different coming from Melanie. I liked it.

"Is that right…?," trying to keep my mouth from gaping open in amazement. I could feel my palms begin to perspire and a drop of sweat form on my brow.

"Maybe? I guess we'll just have to wait and see…," she said as she rolled away toward the rink. I stood there looking like a disappointed kid that had been told they couldn't go outside in the rain to play.

Although I was shocked and in disbelief, I wanted to know more. I was so excited about my conversation with Melanie, I had to tell the crew.

"Hey fellas! Meet me by the pinball machines," I exclaimed.

"Yo! Guess who I just talked to?" I shared with enthusiasm.

"Who? Frank's momma?" Lewis jokingly replied.

"Hey man…forget you! Leave my moms out of this…and I won't have to bring your momma into it," Frank jabbed back.

"Aww… that was a good try but your insults are terrible. But anyway, back to you Jay. Forget about this guessing game stuff…who were you talking to?," Lewis asked.

"Melanie…" I replied with a huge smile and slanted head.

"Whatever. I don't believe that one bit. Melanie? She's one of the finest girls at school. How did you pull that off?," Lewis asked.

"I don't know how it happened, all I know is…it did. And she said that she may be interested in me," I shared my ego growing by the minute.

"Oh hell…you just making stuff up now," Lewis commented.

"Naw…he's not. I overheard the conversation for myself. He's not lying," Chris assured.

"Well what's up with her friends? Let's go over and talk to them," Lewis suggested.

Although I was a little apprehensive, I agreed and we headed over to Melanie and her friends for (thinking positive)…a good conversation. As we approached, I saw two of Melanie's friends, Abbey Warner and Tamika Lorie, whispering something in each other's ear. Viewing myself as a key piece in this bridge between friends, I spoke to Melanie first and then greeted the rest of their group. After that, I focused my attention on Melanie and let everything else fall into place. Lewis started a conversation with Tamika, while Chris chose to converse with Abbey. And Frank, as usual didn't have a problem sparking a conversation with the ladies, began talking with Jennifer Tempest.

Evidently, our dialogue was enough to keep their attention because we talked and skated with them for the rest of the night, until it was time for my mother to pick us up. After saying our "goodbyes" to the girls, the crew and I made our way to the front entrance to locate my mother's car in the parking lot. After we spotted it we walked over and got in one by one. I had a strange feeling that something wasn't right but couldn't place my finger on it. A few moments later it struck me like lightening when my mother asked one simple question, "Where's Eric?"

Eric Thomas

8 CONFESSIONS OF CONVICTION

We looked around at each other in my mother's car, and trying to come up with an explanation for our missing friend. We couldn't come up with anything.

"Ummm…we don't know where Eric is?," I said speaking for everyone.

Once my mother heard the news, she led us on what would soon turn out to be an unsuccessful mission. We searched the skating rink, asked our classmates and chaperones for tips, and scoured the skating rink to no avail. There was no sign of Eric. We realized that we had done all we could there, and my mother decided it was time for us to make the very difficult task of contacting Eric's mother. We were all staring at my mother as she dialed the telephone number. What happened to our friend? He just disappeared? So many things were going through my mind and we were all afraid of Mrs. Thomas's reaction to Eric's disappearance. As we stared adamantly at my mother we expected a look of disappointment, but we were shocked and relieved at the sigh of relief that came over her.

"Oh, so…he's there with you?," my mother asked, "Well that's a huge relief off my shoulders." The guys and I stood around looking confused at one another trying to make sense of what we had just overheard. "Oh, I see…yeah…I understand how that could have made him feel uncomfortable and left out," my mother stated. "Ok, well I'm glad to hear that he made it home and is safe. Take care and I'll see you on Sunday. Ok, Bye."

When my mother hung up the phone with Mrs. Thomas, she told us to head toward the car and wait for her while she alerted everyone who was temporarily inducted into the "Find Eric" search party that he was home safe with his family. During my mother's brief absence, all of us expressed our confusion about why Eric would leave us, and the party, without telling us. Although we continued to hypothesize about why, it was abruptly halted when my mother got in the car and proceeded to drive off. Driving in the direction of our homes, my mother explained to us why Eric left without informing us. She said Mrs. Thomas said he felt left out and how we should be mindful of how we treat one another, because the average person won't have too many "genuine" friends in this life. She informed us that when you have an individual you can call a "friend," you should make sure that person is never taken for granted. After my mother's explanation, about how Eric felt isolated by our actions, we thought about the reason for Eric's early departure from the party and it all made sense. All of us, unknowingly, made Eric feel isolated by our actions. Drifting into a deep trance, I began to organize the series of events that led to Eric's feelings of isolation.

For starters, Eric had always been shy when it came to being with crowds and in gatherings as far back as I can remember. Being at a skating rink in front of so many peers was definitely not the ideal situation for him to begin with. Secondly, when we all went over to Melanie and her friends to join them, Eric was pushed to the back of the crowd. There were five of us and only four of them which made him the odd man out. Not to mention, any memories of Eric being around me at the skating rink became rather hazy once Melanie was in the picture; and I believe this could be applied to all of us, even Frank. I guess Eric sort of drifted into the background and didn't see the reason for staying around people who forgot he was there.

After everyone was dropped off at their residences, my mother and I coasted toward home. As we drove, like we did on many occasions, we had a heart to heart conversation. My mother admitted to having gone through a similar situation in her adolescent years when a few of her childhood acquaintances, deserted her at a drive-in because they didn't have enough room for her and the three other boys her acquaintances had eyes for. The only difference between my mother's experience and Eric's was the people she was with were acquaintances. Eric was our brother. My friends and I honestly didn't mean to make Eric feel isolated, but my mother's old acquaintances did. Even though the situations weren't exactly the same; the principle applied, making people feel isolated, especially your friends or acquaintances can cause serious and lasting wounds. This "bottom-line" principle would resonate with me the rest of the weekend.

On Monday morning, we all commenced to our daily routine. When I arrived at the usual rallying point by the fork in the road to meet up with

Frank and Lewis, I suggested that we apologize to Eric as a group and let him know that we never meant to make him feel left out.

"I know what you mean and all, but I don't think we need to do all of that. I mean, yes, it was messed up that we didn't notice him missing earlier but it's not our fault that he's scared to talk to girls. After all, we didn't leave him… He left us." Lewis expressed.

"So you're saying that we shouldn't apologize?" Frank responded.

"No, I'm not saying that. You all feel free to do what you want." Lewis stated.

Although Lewis had a point, I still felt like apologizing to Eric would be the right thing to do. Throughout the school day I saw Eric several times, but I found myself hesitating to apologize for the role I played in the confusion on Friday night; mainly, because it kept feeling like the wrong time to bring it up. So I resisted and planned on pulling him to the side at the end of the school day to offer an apology before we met up with the guys.

Walking from class to class, room to room, and teacher to teacher, I couldn't help but notice that something felt strange about how the day was unfolding. I didn't know if it was the fact that I knew today the guys and I were going to meet for our reading club, or if it was the subconscious feeling of guilt I had for what I did to a friend, and a brother. In light of my drifting thoughts, I was jerked back to reality by a school bell. To my surprise, I looked at Ms. Wheeler's clock and confirmed it was in fact 3pm.

Exiting the classroom, I could see Eric in the distance on the way to my locker. I wrestled with the idea of apologizing to him before stopping at my locker, but before I was able to decide, Eric stepped into the restroom. I hurried to my locker to change out my books and prepared myself to give the apology I've been planning to offer Eric since yesterday. After I closed my locker and waited for Eric to come out of the restroom it was to no avail. I never saw him make an exit. I decided to head into the restroom myself and see if everything was ok. Once inside – there was no trace of him. I walked out of the restroom, feeling rather bewildered, I headed toward our usual meeting place. When I arrived I saw everyone but Eric.

"Did any of you see Eric pass by? I saw him go into the restroom by my locker but he never came out. When, I went in to check on him he wasn't there. I thought I might have missed him or he may have passed by without me seeing him," I explained.

"Nope, he didn't come by here….I've been out here the whole time because we played kickball outside in gym class today," Frank responded.

"Hmmm, that's weird. I wonder what happened to him?," I said perplexed.

"Well, I guess it's official…Eric's nickname from now on is 'disappearing act' because lately he's been able to vanish into thin air," declared Chris.

"Ha, ha! You're exactly right…Mr. Disappearing Act has been stalling out on us. He needs to teach us some of those magic tricks," Lewis said jokingly trying to find humor in the situation.

We continued to joke about the whole ordeal for another five minutes or so, until it turned into a "jokes session" with one another.

"Oh man, you should've seen this guy trying to be Mr. MVP during the kickball game today. Notice I said…trying…because someone caught every ball he tried to kick for a homerun," Chris sparingly voiced while summarizing Lewis' performance in the game.

"Whatever man! If I would've worn my other shoes…they'd still be looking for the ball," Lewis retorted in an attempt to save his self-started reputation as a sports-star.

"Ah man, whatever! It had nothing to do with your shoes. Wait a minute…Frank, don't you and Lewis wear the same type of shoes in gym?" Chris asked.

"Yep!" Frank eagerly answered.

"I thought so," Chris replied.

"So, what's your point?" Lewis questioned.

"Frank, didn't you kick a homerun?" Chris asked Frank.

"I sure did!," Frank responded.

"Well Lewis…there you have it," explained Chris.

In the midst of all the jokes, somehow Frank spotted Eric peaking around the front entrance of the school.

"Eric?!?! Is that you? Why are you trying to hide? Are you trying to avoid us?," Frank inquired.

"I didn't really see the point of attempting to hang around people who could care less about whether I came around or not," he shouted back as he came around the corner.

I flashed Lewis a stern look in an effort to get him to change the expression on his face. I wanted to take the opportunity to respond and apologize for what happened at the skating party. "I guess we kind of deserved that, but let me be the first to say that we didn't mean to make you feel left out. Yes, we did get distracted at the party but we never intended to make you feel isolated from the group. You're one of us…you're crew for life whether you want to be or not."

"Yeah man," everyone agreed. "That's really reassuring to hear, because I felt like a black sheep all weekend and all day today," Eric responded with a growing smile he tried hard to hide.

"As long as you have us…you'll never be alone," Frank assured.

"Oh my goodness…someone please save me from all this sensitivity!," Lewis spouted.

"Whatever Lewis, you know you feel the same way. Everyone ignore him," said Frank.

"Frank is right, as long as we have each other….we'll never have to worry about being alone. We're brothers forever!," I said trying to dissolve a dispute before it started.

After finally being able to reconcile with Eric, individually and collectively, we finally left Piedmont Elementary and were in route to the *The Reader's Circle*. Walking toward our destination, I began to think about how happy I was that the whole group was together and on good terms again. When we arrived at the circle of big oaks – there seemed to be a gloom of the afternoon sky. It put me in the mind of a great milieu for a horror film; or it could just be that I'm really fond of scary movies. At any rate, and like clockwork, we all took our normal positions. Before we delegated which book would be presented for the evening, and who would present it, Eric surprisingly said that he had something to say.

"I thank you all for your apologies, because I didn't think any of you would miss me either way, but I'm glad to know the truth now. Actually, I would like to thank you guys; because after walking home from the skating rink, I decided to finish the book I was supposed to read for our meeting a while ago. If you don't remember, the name of the book was *Invisible Man* by Ralph Ellison. Thinking about how I was feeling that night made me want to go and start reading it again. Just like the main character in the book, sometimes I feel like I'm invisible to the world because of the way I'm treated. Sometimes I feel like I want to yell for people to listen to me and see me at times. Instead of shouting, I just stay to myself. Before you all spotted me coming out of school today, my plan was to avoid the four of you and to save myself from ever feeling the way I felt on Friday night ever again. But after hearing what you had to say, and thinking about everything on the way here, I realize it's not fair to do that. I should've never left like that; the only reason I left the skating rink was because everyone had someone to talk to but me. I knew that none of you recognized it; and if you did, I knew at least one of you would have made fun of me," Eric explained.

Eric's commented sparked several statements; "It wouldn't have been like that", "I didn't look at it like that", "That was the reason?", "You should have said something instead of just leaving", etcetera.

"I understand exactly what you mean. I feel helpless sometimes too." This statement brought everyone to a screeching halt. As if the whole conversation was placed on mute, everyone looked at Chris with a puzzled look. Not only was Chris one of the most popular students at school, but he excelled in everything he did.

"Feel helpless sometimes... Are you serious?! You get a lot of attention, I've never heard anyone say anything negative about you, you have both of your parents, and your family is close. Everyone loves you. If anyone out of this group could honestly say that, it would have to be me" Lewis exclaimed.

"And that's what makes it so frustrating! I know everyone thinks that and people don't take my feelings seriously anytime I express them; that's why you never hear me say how I really feel...because I know no one would take me seriously," Chris responded.

Although we were still caught off-guard by Chris' statements, we really couldn't challenge him. We tried to think of times where we could challenge what he was saying but we had nothing to offer.

"Now that you mention it...I really can't think of a single time when you've told us how you feel. Come to think of it, you always seem to fade into the background," I acknowledged trying to recall examples of times I could recall him doing such a thing.

"I believe you're exactly right, Jay. He does always seem to become a chameleon when we start talking about how we feel about things," Frank conferred.

"On second thought...he really does. Why Chris?" Lewis asked.

"Well, for the same reason I was thinking about holding back what I just opened up about. Because as soon as I said what I said to Eric, Lewis came back with how hard it is to believe that I feel the way I do about feeling helpless. So, instead of always getting that response out of people...I would rather just keep it in," explained Chris.

"So basically, you don't want to talk about how you feel because of what others may say?" Frank asked.

"Yes and no... For one, I don't think people would take me serious because they think my life is perfect. And for two...I don't think it would change things, so I just keep it inside," Chris explained.

"Wow! Thanks for trusting us enough to share how you feel. To tell you the truth, it seems like you've felt this way for a long time. Not that I'm trying to meddle, but what made you want to tell us now?" I asked.

"Awe, come on James....I finally found enough nerve to tell you this much; and now you want me to tell you everything?" asked Chris.

"No, I'm not asking you to be an open book...I'm just curious about what made you choose to bring it up now. I'm just trying to understand my brother," I declared.

"I hear ya, I feel like I have said enough but if you aren't going to let this go, and eventually bring it up again… I'll answer your question" Chris stated. "Honestly, that book brought it out of me" he continued.

"Uh, what book?" Frank asked.

"The book I got from Eric to read…the real reason why we're out here in the first place. It's called *Fences* by August Wilson," *Chris* explained.

"So…are you gonna let us know what it's about?" Frank asked jokingly.

"Well, I was planning on it if you give me a chance to think out my thoughts…dang" Chris answered. "*Fences*" was really a play about an over bearing and self-centered father that caused a lot of confusion in the lives of others around him. The part of the story that hit close to home for me - came through one of the father's sons in the book named Cory. Cory had dreams of his own, but his circumstances forced him to pursue a life based on someone else's goals. And that's exactly how I feel most of the time! Don't get me wrong, I love playing sports because it gives me a chance to release some of my inner-frustrations, but every now and then I don't know if I'm active in sports because of my father or because I really want to. At times I wonder what my life would be like if my father did something else for a living."

"Dang, I never thought things were that way. Because on the outside looking in, it seems like you have the perfect life – both of your parents are still together, you're popular, and you're smart," I stated.

"Right… I don't mean any disrespect to anyone out here, but out of all of us, I assumed you had the best home situation out of all of us," Frank chimed in.

"Wait a minute…before any of you takes my comments and run with them. Let me clarify. I'm not complaining about my life, because I have two wonderful parents that try their best to make sure I have everything I need and that I want for nothing. What I'm saying is - it's tough feeling like you were only put on this earth to live out someone else's life or continuing a legacy that you've never asked for. That's all I'm saying," Chris interceded.

"Well at least you have someone that is available to you when you need them and pushes you to do your best. If it wasn't for the stories y'all share with me, or the very few individuals that acknowledge my existence, I would accept the fact that all hope was lost" Lewis shared.

"How do you figure that…at least you have a father" Frank interceded.

"You're right…I do have a father; but one that I never see. I know you don't have a father and all, but at least you have people physically there for you. My father and I live under the same roof and I may see him once or twice a day…if that. While you all spend time with your families on a regular basis, imagine if you didn't have those moments. How would you feel then?" There was a long pause "Right. You'd feel alone like I do!" Lewis exclaimed. "Man, I'm telling ya…sometimes I wish I was never born, because I don't even think I'd be missed."

"You're acting like none of us are sitting here," I commented in disbelief.

"I wasn't trying to offend any of you…I'm just sharing my thoughts. Since everyone else is opening up about their feelings - I felt compelled to follow suit," Lewis replied.

"And I'm not saying that you were wrong in doing so. What I was saying was in response to the comment you made about thinking that you wouldn't be missed. Just like I told Eric - if any of us left the group, that person would definitely be missed," I expressed back. "You aren't alone so stop thinking you are."

Lewis Porter

9 DISENCHANTED BELIEFS

As the night continued to swallow any remnant of daylight, the group's conversation didn't suggest any sign of coming to a close. Normally, we would only discuss one book per gathering; but I think tonight we decided without saying that we were going to make an exception.

"So Lew, what book did you read?" I asked, hoping he would open up even more.

"*Native Son*, by Richard Wright; why do you ask?" Lewis questioned.

"Well, judging from how this meeting is going…I think it would only be cool for you to share what you felt about the book" I responded. Little did he know I had read the book but I wanted to make sure that Lewis was ok based on his summary of the book.

"Alright, alright. Ok, so…the main character of the book was this dude by the name of Bigger and the storyline attempted to take the reader on a journey to locate the reasons Bigger was the way he was. Honestly, this book didn't turn out to be what I thought it would be; but it did spark something in me that I didn't know was there," Lewis explained.

Thinking about what I remembered from the book, I was afraid to ask 'why'. But before I could get the question out, Frank did it for me.

"What did you originally think it was going to be about, and what did you discover?" Frank asked.

"Well, to be honest, I thought it was going to be based on a character like in the book James read. You know…someone that stood up for his self for the right reasons. But to me, the main character of the book I read, Bigger, wasn't as honorable. As far as the feeling that it brought about in me, it was a certain level of empathy and fear. I empathized with him because of his living conditions; because the way I feel about my living conditions at times are similar. The part that scares me is…umm….is…" Lewis spoke hesitantly.

"What? Quit stalling on us…it's cool. Be open" Chris encouraged.

"Well, that I could possibly turn out to be like Bigger because of our similar conditions." Lewis responded faintly holding back tears. "Ok, that's enough of this…I'm done. It's late and I have to get back home."

"Lewis, come on man….you can't just bail on us like that," I contended.

"Right…we've all shared things out here that were hard for us to say. But we didn't walk out on anyone," Chris supported.

"I don't care, because I'm not you and you're not me," Lewis rebutted back as he stood up and began to walk away from the circle.

"You know what Lewis…there's gonna come a time when you won't be able to run away from your problems any more. Then what you gonna do?," Frank shouted at Lewis, which only fell on the ears of an empty forest. Lewis was already gone…physically, mentally, and emotionally.

Although Frank was right, we looked at each other and tried to pick up the pieces of what just occurred. Rather than following Lewis away I made a suggestion.

"Fellas before you decide to leave can we finish the discussion of the book? Personally, what I believe Lewis meant by saying he 'didn't want to turn out like Bigger' was that in the book Bigger ended up acting out his frustrations about his living conditions and how his life was and wound up murdering an innocent person…actually two innocent people," I explained.

"Yeah James you're right; lets continue the discussion of the book. Especially since Lewis will most likely continue to run away from his problems; it seems like we are the only ones he would let in enough to help him" Frank concurred.

"Why do you think Lewis is scared of that? This guy 'Bigger' and Lewis are two totally different people. I think Lewis is thinking way too much about the situation, because where would he get the idea that he would murder somebody" Chris asked?

"Well, I don't believe he is afraid of murdering someone, but I think he is more frustrated about his situation and doesn't know what to do to change it. I think it will take him a long time to be comfortable with who he really is and the situation. I don't think he is afraid. I think he's just frustrated with himself and his circumstances," I suggested.

Our meeting continued for a little while longer until we all decided to head back home; because we were sure our parents had started to wonder about our whereabouts. On our way out, I could swear that I heard the faintest sound of what seemed to be someone crying. I stopped in my tracks, and against my better judgment, I followed the cries. I told the others to wait for a moment but I was sure they would come following behind if I took too long to search around. Right before turning around and trying to convince myself that I was only imagining things, I saw two shoes huddled behind several large leaves hanging from a tree branch that almost touched the ground. During my brief pause, I discovered my suspicions to be true, when I separated the leaves - they uncovered a very familiar face. It was Lewis.

"Hey guys…go ahead without me. I think something fell out of my pocket back by the oak tree I normally sit under. I'm going to head back and grab it," I told the others.
"Go back on your own, as dark as it outside right now? Forget about it! We're coming with you," Frank insisted.
"Thanks, but I'll be ok," I firmly reassured.
While trying to decide whether to leave me behind or to come along with me anyway, Chris finally said, "Ok, you can go ahead and be 'Mr. Big Bad Man' if you want to; I'm heading on back home. Besides, you all know how my mother can be at times."
"I guess I'll go ahead and follow him, seeing how you want to go back by yourself," Frank added.

After we parted ways, I took several paces and a few glances back to ensure they were in fact serious about going home without me. I stepped behind the nearest tree until I felt the coast was clear before heading back to where I found Lewis. He appeared to be very upset.

"Ay man, what are you doing?" I asked.
"Nothing Jay…just mind your business," Lewis responded.
Surprised by his response, I asked, "Why are you still trying to act so hard when it's obvious you're not ok?"
As Lewis tried to tell himself I was wrong, all he could mutter was, "Whatever Jay…you don't know what you're talking about."
"Fine, if that's the way you want it – I'll leave. I guess you like to be alone even though you don't have to be," I angrily spouted back.
Although I didn't really want to walk away, I told myself to keep going; until I heard him yell, "Jay…wait a minute, don't leave. My bad – I didn't mean to talk to you like that," Lewis apologized.
"Thanks for the apology, but why do you always talk to people like that?," I asked as I turned around.

After pausing to think, Lewis answered, "I don't know? Well, yes I do. If I say this you have to promise me that you'll never repeat it to anyone; especially to any of the guys".
"Ok, your words will be safe with me" I responded ready to prove my trustworthiness.
"Honestly, I do it to…protect my feelings. Because my older cousin Malik once told me, 'people respect individuals they fear, and they will be less likely to bother the ones they fear'" Lewis explained.
After taking a moment to process Lewis' words, I replied, "Now it makes sense, and I see why you've always been so relentless in the past with others. But I must ask 'why are you that way with us; especially when we consider each other to be brothers?'"
Stumped by the inquiry, Lewis finally responded, "Hmm…I don't know? I've never thought about it like that. I didn't mean any harm by it, but I guess I just kind of got used to it."
"Well, let me enlighten you - it does harm us at times. Especially, Frank" I explained.
"Yeah…I know. It's so easy to ruffle Frank's feathers I can't help myself but I get what you're saying," Lewis responded.
"Ok cool, that's great to hear. But enough with that, let's get back to the reason you're hiding in the first place," I invoked.
Lewis, obviously uncomfortable by the question, looked at the ground and took a couple of deep breaths before answering, "Well, every day I look into the mirror…I hate the truth I see."
"What 'truth' are you referring to?" I asked.
"The truth that every person I've heard, read about, or know who fits my background – is destined to fail. And I grow more and more frustrated with that idea every day because I want to experience something better than what everyone and everything suggested awaits when I get older," Lewis shared.
Overcome with empathy, I tried to respond in the best way I knew how, "In my opinion, we didn't choose our circumstances but we can choose the way we handle them," I suggested.
"Wow, I never looked at it like that. Maybe that's been my problem all along – the way I've been looking at things. I'm telling you Jay, in all sincerity, you really have a gift."
"Thanks Lewis, but I'm only sharing something that was taught to me," I assured.

I helped Lewis to his feet and we headed toward our normal entrance into the woods. Before we could get very far, from out of nowhere, Eric appeared. It looked as if he had pulled the same move on me I tried to pull on him and the other guys.

"Eric, what are you still doing out here; were you eavesdropping on our conversation?" Lewis asked.

"Wait a minute before you go over the top, I didn't want to leave James out here by himself especially after what happened at the party," answered Eric.

"I appreciate that Eric, but it does feel like you were spying on us," I kindly admitted.

"I'm pretty sure it may appear that way, but that's not what I did at all. I overheard a little bit of the conversation then I walked away to where I'm standing now," Eric tried to reassure.

"So what did you overhear? And you better not lie!" Lewis asked in a confronting manner grabbing Eric by his triceps.

"Take it easy Lewis and let go of his arms. Give him an opportunity to answer," I insisted.

While Lewis slowly unleashed the grip he had on Eric, he firmly repeated, "So, what did you hear Eric?"

"I just heard everything up to the point when you asked James not to repeat something, and then I walked off," Eric answered.

"Quit lying! I know you heard more than that…tell the truth!" Lewis demanded.

"I'm not lying! Honest…that's all I heard," Eric reaffirmed.

I knew Lewis didn't believe Eric so I tried to make peace in the situation, "Lew, just let it go. If he said he didn't hear anything else, then he didn't hear anything else. Right…Eric?"

"Well…ok, I did hear more than that. But I didn't mean to," Eric admitted giving in.

"I knew you were lying!!" Lewis shouted angrily.

I tried to move in between them as fast as I could like a referee with a whistle, because I knew Lewis was about to go after Eric, "Whoa....whoa…Lewis, keep cool and relax for second. It's not that serious," I tried to convince.

"What do you mean it's not that serious?! I just shared some serious stuff with you in confidence…or at least I thought. And Eric was listening the whole time" Lewis explained.

"Ok Lewis, you may be right but you know Eric didn't mean any harm. Did you Eric?" I said in hopes of settling Lewis' anger.

"Of course I didn't mean any harm! The only reason I stayed around and listened as long as I did was because I couldn't decide if I should interrupt your discussion. I kept waiting for the best opportunity to step in, but it never seemed to come," Eric confessed as he came clean.

"Well, like I asked before – what all did you overhear?" Lewis repeated.

"Honestly…I kind of heard the whole conversation" Eric said with a grimace.

"THE WHOLE CONVERSATION???" Lewis asked rhetorically. "I'm about to bust your head wide open!!"

"LEWIS! Calm down before you do something you'll regret. Remember what we just finished talking about," I exclaimed.

"Jay man, get out of the way. Wait a minute…as a matter of fact, this is the main reason I didn't want to say anything to begin with. I should've just let you walk off in the first place," Lewis yelled.

"Whatever – I know deep down you don't mean that," I remarked.

"The hell I don't!! I do mean it!" Lewis exclaimed.

After going back and forth a few more times, and several promises of confidentiality were made, Lewis finally came down from his mountain of anger and apologized for some of his outburst. Actually, the three of us eventually revisited the topics Lewis and I had discussed prior. I didn't know about Lewis and Eric, but I greatly benefited from our conversation that night; and just like we agreed…I intended on keeping everything that was discussed strictly between the three of us. That night certainly signified what the real meaning of our meetings at the big circle of oaks was really about, strengthening brotherly-bonds and lending each other a helping hand, and most importantly seeing the hope in each other's lives.

The Seasons of Life

10 MODIFICATIONS OF LIFE

My friends and I continued to meet at the big circle of oaks, day in and day out, for the next six years; all the way through middle school and high school. During that span of time, all of us experienced a plethora of changes and transformations; everything from our personalities and physical appearances to the dynamics of the group. Frank ended up joining our church's youth choir; and on occasion, he would share a few songs with us. Personally, I thought it was a great addition to our regular gatherings, but it took others some time to get used to it. For Eric, I don't know if the reconciliation from the whole skating rink ordeal, or the private conversation Lewis had with him and me after one of our meetings but, he seemed to be coming out of his shell more and more. So much so, that he led a group of students from school to a victory at a state-wide science bowl; he came a long way. Lewis continued to be the same old Lewis; he always seemed to be in trouble for doing something, but he would always get out it one way or another; I guess it had to do with what my mother deemed as charisma, but who knows? And Chris, he seemed to be growing taller by the day. In addition to his rapid development, his reputation began to spread outside of Piedmont County to some surrounding states after winning a few major competitions in the region. As far as myself, I tried to maintain a low profile and did just enough to get by because I was more than ready to move to another school; something different than what I had experienced thus far. Finishing out our 6th grade year, we also kept our routine for meeting at *The Reader's Circle* and we remained close friends throughout the summer until we made our transition from elementary to junior high.

The junior high years were extremely tough for all of us. It was during this time we experienced puberty and were introduced to new surroundings and challenges. For the most part, we all remained pretty close; but since junior high seemed to have yielded us a little more freedom and opportunity to explore new friendships, we took advantage and branched out from our comfort zones. Chris and I got into a few fights, not with each other but a few fellow peers. I guess we did it to prove that we could handle our own and stand up for ourselves. I would have never admitted this to anyone at the time, but neither one of us was big on fighting; however, both of us knew the option of backing down wasn't really an option. Frank…well, let's just say he was bullied regularly, but it never broke him down. Although the rest of us tried to come to his aide on a few of those occasions, it was impossible for us to always be there for him. Lewis developed other circles of friends until he realized the circles he ran with were really not friends at all. Due to this, we could all sense him pulling away from us but we didn't say anything to him about it because it would only cause him to drift further away. So, we continued to extend our friendship to him even though we knew our brotherly bonds with him continued to become more and more distant. Lewis' childhood desires of becoming a policeman slightly changed after several unfriendly encounters of unjust treatment during this time. I can recall like yesterday him telling us about a time when a policeman stopped him while he was walking one Saturday evening to meet his cousin at a restaurant. He said that the policeman pulled up beside him and flashed his lights in his face then asked him for his ID. Then after he gave it to him the officer commented that there must have been a problem because Lewis "wasn't in the system." Even after all of that, the policeman continued to harass him for another ten minutes until another police officer pulled up and told him to stop bothering "that little black kid." Lewis' feelings about police quickly changed from friend to foe. Eric pretty much kept the same modus operandi and continued to be viewed as a nerd or 'good boy.' Middle school was extremely rough for him, in regards to interacting with peers, but he seemed to find refuge in his studies. He always seemed to be in the top 3 of our class according to grades.

After we finally made it to high school, things drastically changed. Freshman year, Lewis proved to us that he still didn't learn from his mistakes, and continued to run around with the wrong crowd. He even went so far as to get arrested for being in concert with a few of his buddies after they robbed a local check cashing store on the other side of town. Chris was really coming into his own as a sports star in football, track, and played in a basketball league. For us it was great, because we knew that anywhere we went with Chris…warm hospitality was sure to follow. Me, I pretty much stayed to myself unless I knew you. However, since it always seemed that I knew someone from every little click or group of friends…I pretty much knew at least a little bit about everybody. Frank was ALWAYS around the girls, although some of them thought he was scared of them because he never tried to pursue anything with them. They would soon discover how wrong their speculations were when they saw him on dates with a different girl every other week. To us, it was like girls would easily drop the defenses they held up to us and welcome him with open arms. We always wondered, "How does he do it?" Eric, he played in the band and befriended others that Chris, Lewis, Frank, and I would have never be known to associate with. But then again, most of the school's population felt the same way about Eric; how ironic huh?

Our sophomore and junior years were kind of a blur, but in the midst of it those two specific years seemed to have brought us back together. By this time, all of us had some sort of encounter with the opposite sex. Since we've always been open with each other, Chris, Lewis, and I discovered, coincidently during one of our "club" meetings, that we all lost our virginity during the same week. Eric and Frank were still holding out even though Frank kept a steady girlfriend. Although Lewis would have been completely fervent if he heard me admit this back then, but by far, he was the 'playboy' of the group. Nevertheless, it didn't stop us from giving him flack for all of his fabrications in prior years. Chris had a girlfriend that was known for her academic honors, and was totally his opposite (she was an extravert, and he was an introvert); so it was always interesting to see them interact with one another. I also had a girlfriend. The fellas always teased me about her being a 'good girl'. If you are thinking it's Olivia Summers you would be correct. I guess I could only run away for so long. All jokes aside, I was really fond of her, but from time to time I would express to the fellas, "If you only knew…" just to get them off of my case. Eric, he wasn't too hot with the ladies at all, although he tried. For some reason he just never seemed to fit the description girls our age went for (the girls he liked, didn't like him; and the very few girls that liked him, he didn't like – what a paradoxical?). So, we would often try to poke light of the situation by twisting our fingers behind our backs and explaining how overrated the whole "dating" thing was. I know what you're probably thinking right now, but think about it…would it have been right for us to tell a little fib or share the truth with someone who couldn't handle it?

Senior year was truly a bitter-sweet experience. We had the type of year every senior should have, or at least in our minds, but it was sad because we were all coming to a place in our lives that would change everything we had become so accustomed to. Most of us were moving away to venture off on our own unique paths of life, and we would be apart from each other for the first time. No more hanging out at school together, no more cruising around town in Chris' dependable bucket of a car on the weekends, and even more sadly…no more meetings at *The Reader's Circle.* Although *The Reader's Circle* started on sort of a wimp, it proved to be our very own personal sanctuary away from all of our troubles and concerns. Plus, it served as a place we could go to get things off our chest and mind. It would certainly be missed.

After graduation, I remained in Piedmont and attended the local community college. Although I started strong, I ended up not finishing because of some difficult issues on the home front. One of those issues being the death of my mother; this event in my life almost swallowed me whole. And due to my mental state, I parted ways with Olivia because I didn't want her to suffer from my grief. However, my father and my four friends interceded as much as possible and provided a reason for me to continue living.

Chris went away to run track and play division I football; and during his college experience as a student-athlete, he suffered a career-ending injury but shocked everyone by coming back to exceed everyone's expectations. I continued to follow along with Chris through newspaper columns, magazines articles, television sports coverage, and by personally attending a few of his games and track meets during his four year term of eligibility. Although I still considered him to be one of my closest friends, our friendship didn't seem as strong as it once was because of the new circles his prestige gravitated towards him. Regardless of the change, all that mattered to me was that he appeared to be the happiest he had ever been.

Frank enrolled into a seminary and graduated with a degree in divinity; and just like the gentleman we all knew him to be, he continued to generate an audience wherever he went. During his time at the seminary, I was able to hear several of his public speeches to the seminary's student body and the public at large; and I must admit, every time I heard a message from him I always left the lecture feeling more inspired to live a more righteous life. He was definitely blessed with a gift and was busy sharing his gift with many others. Out of our small circle of friends, he stayed in contact the most. He remained consistent at calling or writing me at least once or twice a month. I don't think he'll ever know how much his kind words at times motivated me to continue striving to do my best in the midst of my personal storms; especially when I had to deal with the passing of my mother.

Eric went to a private university a few hours away from Piedmont where he graduated with honors in architecture. Based on his accomplishments, I often reminded him of the tale of the turtle and the rabbit. Although he wasn't the most outgoing of the group, his persistence awarded him a life-long victory; because in my eyes, and the eyes of all of us, he was a total success and no one could take it away from him. He finally met a woman that was as interested in him as he was in her. But even with that being the case, his friendship with us didn't change like I have witnessed on many occasions when someone is pursuing a relationship. I don't know about you but to me, that made him a very balanced person in my book.

As for Lewis, he started at a small university not too far our hometown then transferred after his sophomore year to a much larger university clear across the country. During that time 'he really lived life' (on and off campus). The bigger the area, the more he could get into. Some of his decisions caused him to frequent the jail system, and almost prison because of an informant's plea deal, but one way or another he would almost always get out on a technicality. I'm convinced that his last stint of legal troubles strongly influenced him to come to his senses. I would like to think that a sort of "tough love" speech I gave him when he was locked up helped open his eyes as well. I'm not sure, but for his sake…I'm glad he changed his ways.

James & Marie

Part 2: Adulthood

11 KOMMEND IN MEIN EIGENES (COMING INTO MY OWN)

Simply reminiscing on the years of my youth, and the band of friends that I've been blessed enough to call brothers, I can't help but be content with my present status and thankful for the life I've had, have, and 'GOD willing' the life I will have in the future. I've had many opportunities to learn about many things due to my various jobs, responsibilities, and circumstances. I've traveled abroad to other countries, and I've also had the pleasure of hearing the life stories of friends, colleagues, and elders; which I have discovered to be a lesson in itself (*a person can learn a lot by taking the time to listen to what other people have to offer, besides…how can humankind help one another if everyone insists on talking at the same time?*). I believed in this ideology so much so, that I'm actually in the midst of completing a book I've been working on for some time now entitled *Echoes of the World.* Actually, I believe these experiences have not only motivated me to search for more knowledge and understanding, along with encouraging me to write a book, but it also inspired me to finally go back to school and graduate with a double major in philosophy and sociology. Although my past work experiences were mostly odd-end jobs, I felt my true calling was to make a difference in this world. What better way to do that than to study about the civilizations and societies of this world. This is the way I have chosen to live my life, and using that thought process is the way I shall remain.

"James, are you ok?" Marie asked knocking softly on the door. I was sitting

in what I call my "thinking room."
"Yeah babe, I'm ok. Just trying to get a few more thoughts out and then I'll be yours for the rest of the evening" I responded hoping to spark a pleasant smile on Marie's face.
"Ok, take your time…I'll be outside in the garden if you need me."
"Ok, I'll come out when I'm done wrapping up these last few paragraphs."

I met Marie several summers ago while taking a much needed walk along the town's riverfront, which I frequented rather often; for me it was very therapeutic and it helped me gather my thoughts. While I was approaching my normal resting spot, I noticed a young woman about 5'7 with curly dark brown hair pinned up in a ponytail and a slim athletically toned body, jogging along the walking path of the riverfront. At the time I didn't want her to notice the sudden nervousness I felt, so I passively said hello accompanied with a pleasant smile. As she passed in front of me I couldn't help but think, "She's absolutely beautiful." This was followed by self-inflected insults of timorous behavior I usually had during situations of this nature, and the forethoughts of regret for not saying anything else other than 'hello.' Just as I drew back to give myself another well-deserved kick to the abdomen, I heard a slight commotion, looked up and saw that she was on the ground. I immediately ran over (totally forgetting about my recent timid thoughts of hesitation) and asked if she was ok. Thankfully, the injury wasn't a serious one…with the exception of her pride. It had turned out that she accidentally stepped on an acorn and slightly turned her ankle. While I assisted her to her car, we had a great conversation. We exchanged numbers and the rest is history. In a few months, I'll have the pleasure of changing my introduction of her from, "this is my fiancé" to "this is my wife." She has truly been a blessing and I thank GOD for her every day.
Doing the best I could to stay focused on the task of placing the finishing touches to *Echoes of the World*, and the words were flowing so effortlessly on the computer screen before me, I could hear the house phone ringing in the other room. Normally, when I am in my writing mode I would just let the answering machine be my secretary and I would return the call when I was done for the day or when I decided it would be better for me to take a break rather than punish a great story or literary work. I didn't pay it any attention and figured Marie came in from the garden to answer it because I didn't hear the standard greeting of my personal automated assistant.
As I continued to type, I heard a light knock at the door. Immediately I knew it had to be something serious. Marie wouldn't bother me otherwise.

"James… I'm sorry to interrupt but it's Frank and he says it's urgent," Marie said apologetically.
"Ok, come on in babe."

Marie opened the door and entered the room with a look of concern. When she handed over the phone, something inside of me tried to counter the situation by suggesting that it was probably not as bad as it seemed. Once I had the phone and Marie turned and headed back towards the door, I knew she would only close the door and listen from the other side.

"Thanks babe", I told her before lifting the phone to my ear. "Frank, how's everything going?" I asked.
"Hey James." Immediately, I knew something was certainly wrong. "Actually things aren't going too well right now, and I'm pretty sure it will be this way for a while" he continued.
"Why is that? What's wrong?!" I questioned.
"Are you sitting down?" Frank asked.
"Yeah… why do you ask?" I questioned once more.
"Well, I received a phone call from my sister and she told me that…" I could hear Frank holding back tears, "…that… Chris shot himself this morning," Frank uttered no longer able to stifle his emotions.
"What?!?! Chris?! Did you say Chris???" I asked in total shock and disbelief.
"…Yes" Frank was finally able to confirm in the middle of his anguish.
I felt a hand on my shoulder; it was Marie. Once I made sure Frank had someone with him, I told him that I'd call him back. I needed to time to process this information. I almost felt like I was dreaming. I couldn't fathom the information I had just heard. I hung up the phone numb. Marie quickly stepped in front of me, wrapped her arms around my head, pulled me to her bosom and said, "It'll be ok. Whatever it is; we'll be ok".

I tossed and turned the whole night trying to keep my mind from racing, I somehow found myself being awakened by the sun beaming in through the bedroom window. Beginning to yawn, I could tell that I woke Marie by the unconscious gesture.

"Hey babe…how do you feel?" Marie asked.
Turning to take a glimpse at my beautiful wife to be, I responded, "I'm ok. I was just laying here trying to remember at what point of the night I finally dozed off. For a while, I didn't think I'd get any sleep. All I could think about when I closed my eyes was the last time I saw Chris and what we talked about. This whole thing doesn't seem real."
"I know…it doesn't seem real at all, but it is," she replied.
"Yeah I know…" I stated still trying to come to grips with the horrible reality.
Pulling Marie close to me, she asked looking directly into my eyes, "What do you feel like doing today?"

Being that it was a Saturday morning, I really didn't feel like doing anything, especially when all I could think about was the fact I didn't have a chance to say goodbye to one of my brothers and one of my best friends; and that I would never be able to see him alive again. But I tried to respond the best I could, "Well, I guess I'll get the house prepared since I'm pretty sure we'll have company here in the next few days. After that, I'll probably go pay Chris' parents and fiancé a visit. Would you like to accompany me?"
"It's about time…I was waiting for you to invite me," she responded showing her big pretty smile, "Of course I will join you - without you there's no me…and without me there's no you. I know our special day is quickly approaching and all, but you're not going to be able to get rid of me that fast. "

I playfully grabbed her and hugged her. In that moment I thought about how, for a just a moment…I forgot about everything going on in my life. If I ever needed confirmation of whether or not I should go through with the wedding or not, I had just received it. Marie was indeed my better three-fourths.
Once we finally got out of bed and helped ourselves to my signature pancakes, eggs and sausage, I started straightening up around the house. I knew Frank loved to scan along the large book collection Marie and I shared, so I made sure to wipe down the bookshelves and slightly pull out the books I thought he might enjoy scanning. Lewis, I knew he would be the first to look through my massive music collection for anything new and give me recommendations from things he'd heard lately. I put the towel and cleaning spray back to use and cleaned around my radio player, stereo, albums, CDs, and speakers. As for Eric, I knew he liked going on the backyard deck and offering compliments about the landscape and Marie's garden – so after I finished inside I headed out back to pick up a few limbs and prune back several of the bushes that occupied backyard space. And lastly, for Chris I would definitely have to re-shelve a couple of items in the garage because I knew he would peek his head in the garage to see what new tool I added to "the man collection." As I walked toward the garage, reality started to set in…Chris wouldn't be attending this gathering. While I tried my best to hold back the tears forming in the corners of my eyes, I couldn't help it…the rivers began to flow. My friend, my brother…was dead and it hurt. All that I could think was, "I never had a chance to say goodbye."

During my emotional tempest, I could hear the sound of Marie's voice calling my name, "James…you have a phone call! It's Lewis!"
"Ok, tell him I'm on my way."
Approaching the steps of the deck, I tried to make sure I wiped away any

remnants of my emotions. I took the phone from Marie with appreciation, "Hello."
"What's good Jay? This is Lewis. I just made it into town and wanted to see if you and the guys felt like getting together tonight at *The Corner Pocket*?" Lewis asked.
"Around what time?" I inquired.
"Let's see…it's around…two o'clock right now. So…how about 7?" said Lewis.
"Ok, I'll be there…thanks for the heads up! I'm about to finish running a few errands before too long. But at any rate – I'll get up with you and the crew later tonight," I confirmed.
"Sounds good my brother…see you then," Lewis responded.

I still had to finish making the house ready for company and make a stop by the Dunn's residence before linking up with the guys. I tidied up a few more things and then proceeded to take a shower and throw on some clothes. While I took a shower in the German-inspired guest-room 'wash closet' or 'WC' for short, Marie occupied the master bathroom. Once we were ready, we walked out of the front door, jumped in the car, and were on our way. Along the way, I stopped at the florist to pick up a small assortment of flowers for Chris' mom and Taylor (Chris' fiancé); followed by a brief sojourn at the local grocery store to pick up some food to offer the family. I guess I called myself trying to simulate the types of thoughtful gestures I remembered people doing when I lost my mother.
After I made the two stops I originally intended to make, along with the several others Marie asked me to make along the way, we began to approach Chris' childhood home. And reality proved too much for me to handle. I pulled over to the side of the road to regain what little bit of composure I temporarily discovered I had, but it was hard to hold on to it.

"Take your time babe. I know it's hard, but you can do this," Marie calmly reassured me.
"Thanks, babe...you know I love you right?" I stated.
"Yep, and you know I love you too" she said returning the sentiment.
Trying to gain back my courage and confidence, I sat up and said (mostly to myself), "Alright…I can do this. If GOD allowed me to make it through my mother's death, I can make it through this too."
"You're completely right. You got this. Now let's go and give Chris' parents some much needed support," Marie suggested with motivation.
"Ok. Thanks, babe. I needed to hear that" I responded.
"No problem. I know you'd do the same for me, right?" She asked.
"You know it," I replied.

Taking my foot off the brakes and tapping on the gas, we approached the driveway and I slowly pulled in. For some reason, I thought the driveway and the street facing the house would be loaded with cars, but it appeared as if they only had two visitors; as we approached two unfamiliar cars in the driveway. Exiting the vehicle, I continued to have an indescribable sense of surrealism. Ignoring it, we continued on our way to the front door and I rang the doorbell. Mrs. Dunn opened the door and threw her arms around me to give me a tight embrace.

"Oh James, it's so good to see you. I'm sorry for the way I am (with tears slowly trickling down her face) but whenever I used to see you, Lewis, Eric, or Frank I always knew that Chris wasn't too far away. I viewed all of you as my sons, and now that…" taking a brief pause in her words, Mrs. Dunn's tears began to swell much more, "…that Chris is gone you all are the very few reminders I will have of my son."

"It's ok, no need to apologize. Because I feel the same way you just said you felt about us…in my eyes, you're my family as well," I explained.

"Thanks James, you and Marie come on in and make yourselves at home," she said.

"Ok but first, Marie and I brought over a few items to help the family out a little bit," I offered.

"Aww…thanks you two. You all really didn't have to do that. Both of your parents did a great job raising you up. I'll go ahead and take that and the two of you have a seat. Can I get either one of you anything; something to eat or drink?" She asked.

I really wasn't in the mood for anything to eat, but I was taught and always told to be polite when visiting someone's home. I agreed to a beverage while Marie offered to accompany Mrs. Dunn and Taylor in arranging the family/friend's gifts of condolence in the next room. Rearing back on the couch in the front room, memories started to flood my mind. The conversations, the games, the secrets, and the many tales the walls of this house could share about the times my friends and I paid Chris a visit seemed to overwhelm me. Before my emotions could become evident, Mr. Dunn entered the room.

"How are you doing sir…considering of course?" I asked.

"Hey James. I'd be lying if I said everything was ok, so I'll just say that I've had better days," He responded.

"I know what you mean. It doesn't seem real." I replied.

"Well, although it's hard to believe…reality holds no punches," He implied.

Visibly, I could see where this conversation was headed and I didn't want to add to the many late nights of sorrow that waited him. So, I tried to change the subject. "So, my father tells me that you've been doing a lot of renovations on the house?" I asked.

"Yeah, the misses always wanted a covered patio so I decided to put that in a few months ago." He responded.

"Whew… I know that was quite a task,"I jokingly commented.

He replied, "Trust me…it was. Chris and I had our hands full for a few weeks. Yep, my son Chris…" before he could complete the sentence, he buried his face in his hands and wept for his son.

Chris' suicide cut us all very deeply and we would eventually have to accept it. While I attempted to console Mr. Dunn with a few sympathetic words and an arm over his shoulder, Marie, Taylor, and Mrs. Dunn entered the room. When Mrs. Dunn saw her husband's condition, her eyes began to swell with tears and took her place at her husband's side.

"Well, we don't want to wear out our welcome. I think the three of you should have some time alone with each other before more people stop by," I said preparing to leave.

"Oh James, the two of you can stay as long as you'd like. The three of us will have plenty of time to be alone and grieve," Mrs. Dunn replied.

"I know, but we're going to go ahead and go. Marie and I are going to get back home and continue preparing for the arrival of guests as well," I shared.

"It's no worry…we understand. Besides, the two of you coming by to see about us has meant more than enough," Mrs. Dunn suggested.

"No problem ma'am…anytime," I responded.

As Marie and I started to make our way to the door, I still couldn't wrap my thoughts around the fact that Chris was really gone. I continued to keep my composure while Chris's parents and fiancé walked us to the door and gave us parting hugs. Walking toward the car I acknowledged the lingering eerie feeling that draped over me like a heavy garment. And on the ride home my mind seemed to still be at the Dunn's residence. Somehow in the midst of my personal tunnel of twilight I started to imagine how my reunion with Frank, Lewis, and Eric is going to be without Chris being present. Regardless of how much I tried to motivate myself and drift away into positive thoughts, reality continued to keep me at bay.

Following our seemingly "casual" drive home, Marie and I decided to have a quick meal with each other before I headed out to meet the guys at the pool hall. I sat the table while Marie prepared our plates in the kitchen. Although every meal Marie made smelled wonderful to me, I couldn't ignore the amazing smell of one of my favorite dishes – liver and onions, carrots, and steamed asparagus.

"Are you trying to persuade me to marry you sooner than expected? If you are you certainly have me. I'll say 'I do' at this very moment!" I said as she approached the table smiling.

Farewell

12 LIFE'S ADJUSTMENTS

After praying over the food, a few laughs, and good conversation, my wristwatch indicated that I had half of an hour to meet Lewis and the guys at the billiards. I cleaned the dinner table and Marie nicely agreed to do the dishes and wipe down the kitchen (*something that I would normally do when Marie cooked; and roles were reversed whenever the position of chef fell on my shoulders*). After a quick shower, change of clothes, and a gentle surprise kiss on the cheek from Marie, I started out the front door and was in route to the pool hall. With each stop light, and every reminiscent childhood memory I passed, the more I wanted to jump out of the current reality and back into the idea that tonight would be a normal meeting of friends that included Chris. But with every mental drift…reality continued to flag me back down to the fact – Chris' suicide was real, and that tonight would be the first time he wouldn't be amongst the crew; or at least, in the physical sense.

When I finally arrived at *The Corner Pocket,* I could definitely tell the effect Chris' suicide had on Lewis. With cigar in his right-hand, sitting on the trunk of a car with his back against the rear window, gazing up into the dusk skies, I could tell it had already been a long night for Lewis and traces of the sun were still peaking from behind the horizon.

For old time sake, and to get a rise out of him, I said in a slightly-elevated and stern voice, “Hey mister, climb down off the car and act as if you have a sense of decency about yourself!”

Lewis had never been a fan of intimidation, he responded as smoke exited his mouth and without moving a muscle, “Why don’t you come over here and make me?”

“Lew, you haven’t changed one bit” I responded.

Slightly puzzled, he sat up and turned his head. Once he noticed it was me, he said, “Ahh, Jay… I thought I was about to have to throw somebody a beating; especially with all the things going through my head right now.”

“I totally understand that…it’s crazy huh? Who would have thought?,” I commented.

"I know right. Every time I think about it I can't seem to wrap my thoughts around what could have been going through his mind," Lewis said.

"Crazy enough, I said the same exact thing to myself earlier. I can't wait until the other two guys get here because I have a strange feeling those thoughts have been going through all of our heads," I responded.

"Forget strange feelings, I'm willing to bet my life on it. Because it seemed to have come from nowhere" Lewis replied. "So Jay, when was the last time you spoke to Chris?"

"I spoke to him like a week before…. Well you know… And uh, he really didn't give me any reason to believe something like this was about to occur. I mean, he did mention that he wished he could have changed the way things had been over the years and that he wished he would've chosen another route than the one he was on, but I didn't think anything of it; because to me, we all had those thoughts at least once or twice" I responded.

"Yeah, I know what you mean. I knew a couple of other people who committed suicide and in both instances no one saw it coming. I just don't understand it, I mean I really don't see what all was wrong with his life to make him want to do something like this. He had popularity, he had friends, he had two caring parents, he graduated from college, and he was helping others. I just don't understand what possibly could have pushed him over the edge like this," Lewis commented.

"I guess when it comes to suicide I don't think anyone sees the signs… They just question if the signs were ever there to begin with" I commented back.

Lewis and I continued to speak about our disbelief of what could've brought Chris to the point of taking his life until our conversation was cut short. Out of the darkness a voice called out, "can anyone tell me where I can find an ugly bald-headed man named Lewis and his big-headed friend

James?" Lewis and I looked at each other and then glanced in the direction of the voice, and we saw Frank and Eric slowly walking up.

"Oh, if it isn't the little fairy and the intellectual" said Lewis.

"Why aren't you amusing... You can actually say two syllable words? I can definitely see the streets have taught you something," Frank responded sarcastically.

"Wow... I see someone has been working on their comebacks," I stated impressed.

"Well I haven't been working on them but when it comes to getting back at Lewis I think it just comes naturally now," Frank smiled.

"So Eric, what have you been up to?," I asked.

"Oh not too much.... Just designing and creating blueprints" Eric answered.

"I hear that, the life of an architect huh? That's good to hear. Well I guess I will be the first one say it is good to see you all. I wish it wasn't under these circumstances, but I am happy to see all of you," I voiced.

Rather than spending the whole night in front of the pool hall we decided to make our way inside. Our conversation continued during our walk in and I went to grab a table and order the first round of drinks for the night. The jokes continued, and showed no signs of stopping; I believe it was our way of dodging the inevitable. We fought it as long as we could but with each round of drinks, the more open we became, and with every ball sent to a pocket, the more the truth motivated us to vent and share our real thoughts. And since Lewis always seem to never be the one to hold his tongue, he sparked the conversation with one simple statement," man, it sure feels weird not to have Chris around."

"As much as I didn't want to admit it, this whole night...whole day rather...has been tremendously unreal. I keep waiting for someone to call and tell me we're all being pranked and that Chris will eventually come out and say I gotcha. I know I'm only fooling myself and that Chris will never come popping out to say it was all a joke; although I wish he would," Frank stated.

"Yeah, I know what you mean... This time life gave us a mighty slap to the face and we can't do anything about it," I added.

"Whoever said life would be easy must have never felt this type of pain," Eric added.

Our dialogue persisted as we went around the pool table sharing our feelings for our lost brother. However, before spending a month's salary on a bar tab, we decided to head back to my place and conclude the evening there. Since Frank and Eric caught a cab to the pool hall and Lewis was in no shape to drive, I asked Eric to drive because he had the least amount to drink. Although Lewis was not a fan of leaving a car behind, one way or another, we convinced him it was the best decision. With each passing stop light nearing our arrival, the more childhood memories seemed to resurface. From the songs on the old-school radio station, to the old hangout spots we used to frequent when we were younger. Then, out of the blue, Eric mentioned something we haven't spoken about in years.

"Ay, are any of you up for stopping by our old spot, '*the reader's circle*?" Eric asked.

"Wow… I forgot all about that place," replied Lewis.

"I think we all forgot about that place. It has been at least 10 or 12 years since the last time we were out there, huh?," I admitted laughing.

"Dang, has it been that long?," Frank asked.

"Yeah it's been at least that long…you all are getting old," I responded.

"Funny…the pot calling the kettle black huh? Hey, how about we go out there tonight… You know, for old time's sake?, Frank suggested.

"I know you playing… There's no way I'm going out there in them woods tonight. That's all you!," Lewis announced.

"I'm dead serious. Come on… for old time's sake" requested Frank.

"Wait a minute… If you're dragging me out there tonight you better run me by the next liquor store. Because I'm not trying to be out there…this late, with you guys, under these circumstances without some kind of chaser; because I haven't been around this much sweetness in a long time," Lewis confirmed while trying throw a witty insult before we started down memory lane.

"Don't worry about that, I gotcha covered. I was planning on pulling this out when I got back home but we can crack it open when we go out there," I affirmed as I pulled out one of our favorite top shelf whiskeys.

"See, that's what I'm talking about. Now I'm down," Lewis stated.

After I was finally able to settle Lewis down and get him on board, we all sat back and began our journey down memory lane; making our way closer and closer to our old place of escape. Although we were accustomed to walking to the circle of Oaks within the forest, we devised a plan that would keep us safe from any curious authorities or nosey citizens. We decided to park at Lewis' place (*since it was the closest residence to our entrance into the forest*) and walk from there. Once parked, we gathered a few items and started on our way. Along the journey we discussed some of the issues we used to talk about when we were together as kids. Some of those memories opened old wounds, and some sparked moments of laughter; however, the feeling of Chris not being a part of the conversation was definitely felt. And oddly enough, I believe Frank and Lewis decided to lay aside their many misunderstandings for the sake of the group. Chris being the one to usually break up a fight between the two, neither one of them wanted to be an enabler for more misery.

At last, we made it to our old entry into the woods. Fighting through the unmanaged and untraveled paths we used to visit regularly during our younger years, memories came rushing back to our minds. Especially, while balancing ourselves as we walked across the big fallen Oak that used to appear much bigger and now our feet seemed too big to plant any secure steps. When we made it to the circle of Oaks, they seemed to have been waiting on us. And without discussing anything, we took our usual spots and positions within the space. Making my way over to the tree that used to fit me perfectly, I was surprised to discover that it still seemed tailored for my body. Frank and Eric got reacquainted with their personally selected trees, and Frank plopped down and sat Indian-style like he used to do back in the day. Eric, being honest with himself, decided to extend his legs and not bring attention to the fact he couldn't sit Indian-style anymore. As for Lewis, he took one look at the tree and the branch he used to sit on and shook his head; then conveyed to us that there was no way…no way…he was climbing that tree, and chose to take a seat on the nearest stump.

"So what you guys think… Does our old spot still seem the same?," I asked.

"For the most part, yes, but in some ways, no" Frank said looking at Eric's stomach, "maybe you should've asked the trees if we still look the same to them," he responded jokingly.

"Oh, so you have jokes? Well some of us have obviously matured, and some of us have remained the same. Besides, it's not my fault if you were the only one who sought security in femininity," Eric said in return.

"Oh man, I didn't see that one coming… Way to go Eric!," Lewis exclaimed laughing.

"Ahh, whatever. You guys are just mad because you can't do the things you used to do…and you still want to. It's okay, everyone has to surrender to Father Time eventually. My time hasn't come yet. Thanks for giving me an example, in you all, of what it will look like when I have to," Frank replied.

"Wait a minute… I know you're not talking about me because I'm still able to sit where I used to sit," I exclaimed.

"I'm saying, because I can still climb up that tree but I'm not about to embarrass myself tonight. I've already had at least a dozen drinks and I'm not trying to face plant if I happen to slip off that branch trying to prove my youth to you or the baby you're carrying with you," Lewis added while throwing a joke at Eric.

"Okay, okay. Before we start down this path again, as we have always done, let us go ahead and stop now because we all know Chris is no longer here to intervene," I stated.

"Yeah, you're right Jay… Chris is no longer here" Frank said.

"Right! He selfishly chose to take his own life rather than to fight and live," Lewis exclaimed.

"Wait a minute. There's no way I'm going to let you talk about Chris like that because none of us knows what he was feeling at the time. Besides, weren't you the one who said in a meeting similar to this a looong time ago that you wished you were never born? So what if we talked about you then like you're talking about Chris right now…. How would you have felt?," Eric asked.

"Naw man, that was completely different. I was a kid when I said that and he was an adult. I don't see the similarities," Lewis answered.

"How is it different? Because I recall that Chris somewhat alluded to the same thing you referred to that night as well…. So how is it not the same?," I asked.

"How is it not the same? Well, I didn't take my life… That's how it's not the same," Lewis replied.

"Well regardless of how you try to separate the two situations, both of you were talking about no longer existing" Frank added.

"Whatever… Either we can move on with this topic or I can move on and go home. You choose'" Lewis jabbed back at us.

"Alright, alright… Before you run away like you always do we'll move on," Frank suggested.

"What you mean by that?," Lewis asked.

"All I'm saying is – when things get rough you always run away. And it's been like that as long as I have known you" Frank replied.

"Run?!?!? When have you known me to run for anybody…or anything for that matter?," Lewis questioned.

"Well, I don't know about running from specific people, but I can name a whole list of things that you have run from" Frank admitted.

Lewis tried to change his stance on the tree and he insisted that Frank should go into detail, "Like what? Name one" Lewis insisted.

"Well, let's see…. I can name one that should suffice. Yourself," Frank replied.

"Myself, what you mean by that?" Lewis asked.

"You run from your feelings. For example, accepting the life you've been given, and more often expressed – from dealing with the issues between you and your father and getting over them," Frank explained.

"Is that right?," Lewis simply replied as he stepped away from the tree and slowly began to walk in Frank's direction.

"Yeah, that's right," Frank firmly stated back.

Before we could react, Lewis dashed toward Frank and landed a nice stern punch to Frank's jaw. Eric and I rushed over to break up the fight, but the damage was already done and there lay Frank on the ground with a bloody nose. While assisting Lewis away from Frank, and Eric helped Frank to his feet, I tried to make sense of what just transpired. I knew tonight's reunion would be cut short; and as much as Eric or I tried to talk Frank out of leaving we knew he wouldn't go for it. He looked Lewis directly in the eyes for a moment and turned around and walked in the direction of the entrance to the forest. Just like a domino would react to another domino tapping it on its side, Lewis watched Frank as he walked off and decided to take a couple of paces away from us to gather himself. During Lewis' short time away, Eric and I briefly discussed how it would be best for Eric to take Frank home and that I take Lewis to his. Eric dashed off to catch Frank as I made my way over to Lewis. As much as I tried to empathize with Lewis, he was mentally unavailable and in a state-of-mind that rendered him unable to reason until he decided to come back from the land of "guilt trip". I decided to walk Lewis home and call a cab from his place, because I knew Marie was most likely already in bed. After the cab arrived to take me home, my thoughts were in full swing. My mind was racing. On one end I was still in denial over a best friend's suicide; and on the other, I was still trying to figure out what happened tonight. As a group, we knew Lewis had a quick-temper and was very sensitive about discussing some topics, but I don't think any of us saw him acting this way towards us…any of us. Before I could come to any form of decent rationalization, I discovered myself at the end of my route. I paid the fair, entered my house, tried my best not to wake up Marie, got ready for bed and told myself that I would tackle these issues another time.

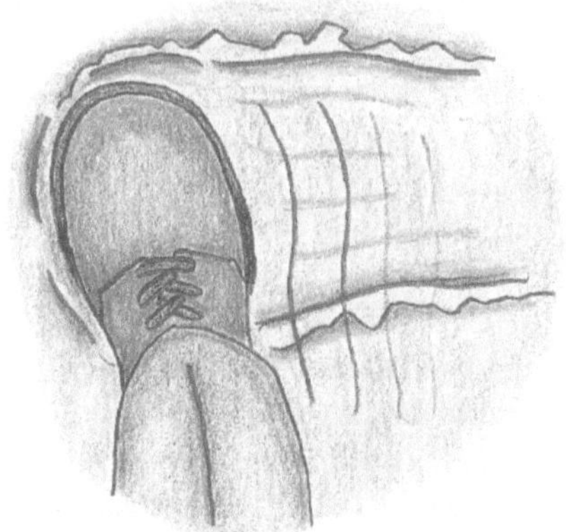

Drawing the Line

13 NO RETREAT, NO SURRENDER

The next morning Marie asked how my night was with the fellas and I tried my best to keep it short. "It was good to see my old friends again." There wasn't much more I could say. For the next three days, I pretty much stayed on an even keel. And then the day of Chris' funeral arrived. I convinced myself that it would probably be at the funeral when Frank and Lewis, would have to resolve what happened a few nights prior. I hoped it would be before this day, but I knew better than to get my hopes up. People's emotions sometime get the best of them, but for the sake of Chris' family and friends, I prayed that those unpredictable people could keep themselves under control at least for a couple hours. I know, I know…everyone deals with grief in their own way but I also believe there's a time for everything…and today was a time for self-control.

After Marie and I were dressed and heading out of the door for the church, not many words were exchanged. And I wasn't sure why; I didn't know if Marie didn't know what to say, didn't know how I would react, or if I felt like talking but it was exactly what I needed to prepare myself for what I knew would be a long day. Pulling up to the church I noticed an abundant number of cars parked in the parking lot and down the street. I always assumed Chris knew a lot of people, but I didn't know he crossed paths with this many. Often times we never know who we may impact as we go about our days; and seeing so many out today proved this to be true. Regardless of the number of people in attendance, I was sure that I'd still be able to find my friends, or at least Frank and Eric. Where Lewis would be was uncertain.

Once the crowd made their way from outside to inside the church, I could not keep my eyes off of Chris' coffin. I kept telling myself that this was just a dream but reality continued to bring me back every time his name was mentioned. Song after song, poem after poem, and Scripture after Scripture went by until I realized it was the part of the service when family and friends could come up and say a kind word or two about the departed. Personally, I hated public speaking; but for a fallen friend…my spirit wouldn't allow me to stay in my seat. Without hesitation I arose from my seat on the pew and made my way to the podium positioned to the right of the coffin. Under normal circumstances my palms would have been wet with perspiration and my voice would have trembled uncontrollably; but in this instance, it was as if someone else was in control and someone was speaking for me. As the kind words flew effortlessly out of my mouth and into the hearts of everyone that knew Chris, I began to feel a burden lifted. I not only shared a kind word or two, but I spoke about the side of the Chris many people didn't know. For the most part people only knew him as a jock. I knew him as a talented individual in life who cared for those who needed someone to care. Continuing to speak heart-felt words of admiration, I sensed an empathetic mist arise from the congregation as if it spread contagiously. I gave Chris a final formal goodbye and returned to my seat. I wasn't sure about everyone else but, the rest of the service seemed to outrun time. The next thing I knew the pastor was reading the prayer. Soon after Frank, Eric, Lewis, and I were signaled along with the other two pallbearers to assemble by Chris' coffin and position ourselves around it. And at the command of the funeral director, we started to lift my friend. With each step, a different set of thoughts came and left as I felt the lifeless vessel slightly shifting inside the coffin; "I wonder if Chris is observing this procession, and if so, what was he thinking? Hopefully, I said enough prayers for the LORD to forgive Chris' soul for taking his own life. I can't believe this will be the last time the crew would officially be together, etcetera."

All of these thoughts continued to run through my head, while the other funeral attendees made their way to various vehicles. Everyone proceeded to follow the police escorts that waited to lead us to the graveyard. From stoplight to stoplight, and through one intersection to the next, we finally arrived at *Peaceful Meadows Graveyard and Mausoleums* where Chris was to be laid to rest. Once there, the crowd gathered at a tent-covered area with an open grave that waited for me and the other five pallbearers to place my close friend's coffin to be lowered to his final resting place. The pastor of our church began to talk and speak about the afterlife while tears from my eyes began to race towards my chin. "Ashes to ashes and dust to dust." The

final words I heard from the pastor.
Shortly after the crowd started to disperse, I told Marie to head back to the church without me. While the diggers prepared to redeposit the dirt back into the hole, I noticed that I wasn't alone. I looked to my left and there stood Frank. I looked to my right and there stood Eric. And with a doubtful turn to see who was behind me, I saw the top of Lewis' head; as it made a slow ascension upward.

"How's it going fellas?" I asked, deeply suggesting some mutual empathy.
"It's going. I can't believe we're really burying my man," Frank answered.
"I know…he's actually gone," Eric said slowly stepping forward.
I paused after hearing my friend's thoughts and looked toward the sky, sharing my own, "This is truly a day I thought I'd never see, but reality has sold me a different story. Bereavement is a hard pill to swallow but you can either accept it for what it is, or choose another route. And considering you all are the closest friends I have…I hope none us will have to experience this ever again for a very long time."
"I totally agree. All we have is one another so we should never get to the point when we feel alone; because none of us are," Frank added.
"I feel the same way Frank…," Eric chimed in.
"Me too," I said slightly turning around towards Lewis. "What about you Lew?" I asked.
After taking a short pause, Lewis replied, "Yeah, I'm with ya. Honestly, until this week…I never really considered how much my actions could affect so many others. So with that said…," slowly moving away from the car, "…yes, I agree. But I'm still having a hard time seeing my partner in the ground like this."
"It's not easy for any of us, but the truth of the matter is…this is definitely real," I offered.
"Very true. I'm telling you guys, the only way I'm getting through this is my faith. Although, he's gone…he still lives on through me. Matter of fact, through all of us," expressed Frank.

After the much needed heart-to-heart, the four of us piled back into the limo and rode back to the church for a little food and social gathering. A couple plates and few sips later, the guys and I decided to meet at my place to continue with our "laugh at few lies & meet on a few truths" conversations. Since Lewis, Frank, and Chris were the only ones with kids, Marie and I told the fellas to bring their wives, fiancés, girlfriends, and kids along. Marie also extended the invitation to Taylor – she was a part of Chris so she was a part of us; at least as far as we were concerned. Once the details were ironed out and the plan was in motion, we left the church together and headed towards my home.

On arrival, Frank and his wife (Sherry), Lewis and his girlfriend (Janine), and Taylor (Chris' fiancé) assembled their children and made their way into our residence as Eric and his girlfriend (Morgan) and Marie and I lead the way. After making the respectful gestures of beverages or eateries, Marie and I made the whole "my place is your place" speech as the guys followed me to the basement for some guy-time; while the ladies and children took over the living and dining areas.
Leading the fellas around, I discussed the upgrades of my humble abode, then slowly transitioned the conversation into the statuses of our current endeavors and life in general.

"So Frank, how's everything going on the home front?" I asked.
Feeling a little 'on the spot' Frank reared back and said, "Well, I have actually been doing a lot of work at the church; like ministering to the youth and others as well. I would say about…two years ago, I started a youth group known as, 'GOD's Vessels.' The focus of the group is centered on living, studying, and carrying out the life of being a vessel to be used by GOD. I must say, there has been a lot of success with the program. Just last week one of the students was given a humanitarian award by our city's mayor for starting a botanical garden in one the most impoverished communities of the city. The mayor said that his efforts were one step in the direction of bringing life back into the community and revitalizing an important environmental structure. Needless to say, the whole experience has definitely been the talk of the program lately. Besides that, just busy being a husband and father. And judging from that little two year old bundle of joy upstairs, I'm sure you can imagine my hands are full. Day care is totally ridiculous, he eats constantly, and he makes me clean up huge mounds of evidence shortly after each meal. But I wouldn't take back experiencing the joy of fatherhood for anything. It has truly been a blessing."
"I know exactly what you mean," Lewis said, with a very adamant expression. "Imagine having two of those, one and three years old. That's why I call them 'double trouble.' But when I'm mentoring the boys at the clubhouse, it makes me appreciate my responsibilities. Because I can just look at any of those kids and see clear evidence that someone didn't step up and take care of their responsibilities as a parent; more specifically…as a father. Honestly, that's what motivated me to name my mentoring group 'Transitions,' because a lot of them missed out on critical development stages when they were younger and current-life stages as well. I think it's so important to me because of all the mistakes I made throughout my life. No one really took the time to lead me. So I guess this is my way of trying to provide for the younger examples of myself, you know secondary-aged male minorities, with a better chance at life and a 'real-life' example of

potential conclusions if they continue to travel down the right or wrong path. So that's what's been going on in my life in a nutshell. But, I must say…you know it wouldn't seem right if I didn't have something going on. Janine is always accusing me of stepping out on her. Now I know, before you all get started... I know I haven't been the most faithful guy but people can change. Although I know I've changed; Janine seems to think otherwise. Outside of that, I'm just trying to take care of business as usual," Lewis added.

"Well, it definitely sounds like the both of you keep busy schedules," I remarked. "Okay, so how about you Mr. Architect?" I questioned while turning to the left to give Eric my attention.

"So, what do I have going on?" He quietly repeated to himself. "Let's see... Okay, I'm in the process of becoming a senior architect at the firm (*Daniels & Rogers*) and I'm also planning on establishing my own private firm over the upcoming year. So I've had my hands full with that for quite some time; plus, Lily and I have been trying to get pregnant the last year or so. Now I know we are friends and all of us can be trusted…" he said looking around at each of us, "... so I am sure what I just told you will remain secret, because Lily doesn't want a lot people to know," Eric stated.

"You can trust us, your secret is safe," we agreed.

"Speaking about secrets… James, what have you been up to? Because one way or another, you always seem to get out of sharing what you have going on…spill it. What's been going on in your world?" Frank asked.

I laughed in response, because he was telling the truth, "Oh, that's cold! Although you may be right; that was still cold… At any rate, I'll go ahead and answer your question. Well, I'm currently writing a book that is almost complete entitled *Echoes of the World* and I am hoping to get it published in the upcoming months. In addition, I have had aspirations of starting an organization that promotes the critical role, or influence, literacy plays in a person's life. I have made a lot of large strides with my efforts, but I'm still kind of concerned about how it will be received by others. I know it is important to me, but I don't know how important it is to others. And of course, last and definitely not the least, I have a big wedding and reception to plan and get prepared for. To be honest, until this point, Marie has done all of that work by herself, so I will be busy with all of the details of that in the upcoming months."

Although I didn't say anything at the time, Lewis' current endeavors brought to life a strong urgency to leave a lasting impression with everyone I would be in the position to help in my day-to-day life. His endeavors also encouraged me to restructure my thoughts of the organization I sought to establish. Instead of limiting the organization to only school-aged students, I should reach out to all ages; K-12, college-aged, adults, and elders. I was greatly appreciative and decided that I would have a more detailed conversation about my thoughts with Lewis at a later time.

Several laugh-induced episodes, almost a liter of whiskey, and at least a dozen stories of reminiscing, later, I noticed Marie standing at the midpoint of the basement stairs.

"I hate to cut this gathering of testosterone short but Taylor and Sherry would like to get the kids to bed before too late," Marie stated.

Although our time together that night didn't go the same distance as some of our old hometown college visits, the time I was able to spend with my brothers was greatly needed. After Marie and I followed out our last house guest, we stepped out of our clothes and into something more comfortable and joined each other in the bedroom. We shared our thoughts about the day and the evening with friends, and complimented each other with a kiss goodnight, turned out the lights, and drifted into our dreams.
The next day Frank and Eric prepared for their trips back to the Midwest with their families, while Lewis and I planned to have a late lunch at *Elmer's* (my neighborhood's local sports bar). During a very brief call that morning, Lewis said he needed to talk to me about something going on back home. Knowing Lewis, it meant he probably had some issues with a female or a personal beef with someone. With him I could never tell, but he's one of my true friends and I didn't have a lot of those. After I made a couple of calls to Frank and Eric before they boarded their planes, I grabbed a few belongings, walked out of the front door, and headed towards *Elmer's*.

Pulling into the *Elmer's* parking lot, I spotted Mr. Porter's truck. After I parked and made my way into the place, I was greeted by a passing waitress; but before she could ask me, "how many?" I spotted Lewis in a booth towards the back of the bar.
"Thanks, but I see my friend, "I told the waitress.
"My pleasure sir, have a nice afternoon," replied the waitress.
Walking toward Lewis I still couldn't figure out what was going on with him.
"What's up Lew? You got me meeting you at a bar…at this hour?" I asked jokingly.
"Whatever Jay, I'll let you get away with that one because you probably still feeling the effects of last night at your makeshift watering hole," he insulted.
Willing to accept that he returned a great gag of a rebuttal, I responded, "I see I'm not the only one with the jokes today, huh?"
"You know I have them for days," Lewis replied.
"I guess you're right. Anyways, what's going on? I mean…if you really

needed to talk about anything, you could have pulled me to the side last night and we could've rapped then," I inquired.

"True…but you know the guys probably would've been eavesdropping from around the corner. Besides, I'm ready to talk about it now so is that okay with you?" He responded in a rather annoyed tone.

Sensing that I offended him, and knowing how sensitive he could be at times, I let my confrontational feelings fall to the floor like a cigarette butt burnt past the brand's logo. "Take it easy…you know I didn't mean anything by it. I was simply reaffirming that whenever you need an ear you have one. And considering that we just lost one of our closest friends rather abruptly – I'm sure you can understand why I would suggest that we no longer put off tomorrow those things, or conversations, we can handle today. That's all," I sternly offered in return.

"I know… My bad Jay, I'm just under a lot of stress right now. I didn't mean to take any of it out on you," he responded.

"No need to apologize. I really didn't take any offense by it. Besides, it's not that serious," I replied.

"Mr. Understandable…as always. That's how I knew I could come to you, if anyone, because I know you keep an open mind about everything and I've never known you to be judgmental," Lewis stated.

"Ok… thanks. But of course, you know I'm trying to figure out what in the world you need to talk to me about," I admitted.

Lewis made several attempts to adjust himself on the table's barstool, finally shared, "Well, this is not easy for me to say… and after I say what I have to say – I hope it makes me feel better; because for the last few days I've really been holding in something that has been weighing me down."

"*Oh my Lord, what is he about to say,*" I silently asked myself, while managing to hide my angst. "Ok. Now, I'm really at a loss. You know I've never been one for these types for theatrics. Come on out with it!"

"Well, James… I had an affair with your cousin Tara and she's pregnant," he stated.

"What!?? Are you serious?? You know if I didn't view you as a brother I would come across this table and snatch you out of that seat, right?" I replied infuriated. Lewis began to laugh. "So, you think just because I said that it still won't happen?," I exclaimed standing to my feet.

"Wait there just a minute, before you travel down that road, I can't hold it in anymore… it was just a joke. Tara and I have never been together; as a matter of fact, the only time I've ever spoken to her was when I was with you," Lewis confessed.

While shaking my head… "So, I take it that you really didn't have anything you wanted to discuss with me huh; you just needed an excuse to get me into a bar at…*glancing down at my watch*…2:30 in the afternoon?" I questioned.

"No, not quite; in fact, I do need to discuss something with you," he insured.
"Ok… What is it then?," I asked stilled rattled by the joke.
"Well, how do you feel about Janine?" he replied.
"Umm, I guess she's ok…at least according to what I know about her," I responded. "Why do you ask?"
"Honestly…" he said while taking a rather generous gulp of beer, "…I ask, because I'm thinking about proposing," he finally divulged.
"Sure, sure… tell me anything. So, how many times do you plan on pulling my leg today," I responded.
"Jay… I'm serious this time! I'm honestly thinking about popping the question when we go to her family reunion next month. I gotta tell ya, Jay; partly based on everything that has transpired over the last two weeks – I've reached a new level of understanding and perspective. I truly realize that I can't take anything in this life for granted, because, like you just brought up, tomorrow isn't promised," he confessed.
"Wow…I never thought I'd see the day when you would be ready for marriage. But first, let me ask you this, 'if the last two weeks never happened could you honestly say, to my face, that you would be ready to marry Janine?," I asked.
"Truthfully, I don't think I would be experiencing the strong sense of urgency I'm feel right now, but it has always been in my plan to eventually marry Janine. The only reason I never voiced it before was because of my own insecurities. I've always doubted if I was husband material or not; and the truth of the matter is that I still don't know, but now I'm willing to jump out on faith and allow it to be what it's going to be," Lewis replied.
"I thought I'd never hear you talk like that; it actually feels similar to how I felt when you were talking about your program last night," I admitted.
"So, what… you didn't think I was capable of coming up with these things on my own?" he asked.
"No, that's not it. It's just that the fellas and I always knew you had it, but we didn't know when you'd finally discover it for yourself," I affirmed. "Honestly, last night you encouraged me to broaden my horizons and expand the audience I intended to reach. Instead of only pursuing the interests of the young. I also need to be cognizant of the elevation of everyone willing to ascend to a higher level."
"That's great to hear, and I'm glad to know that you of all people was encouraged by someone like me," Lewis replied a bit puzzled.
"'Me of all people'… and 'someone like you'? What's that supposed to mean?" I asked.
"Well, you have always seemed to have things in order and stable; even when you were faced with a lot of difficult situations in the past. Me, I know you guys think I'm a live card. So for me to hear you say that I've

helped you is…kind of…surprising," Lewis admitted.
"Interesting… I never thought of myself as someone who has it all together because I definitely don't. I just try to do my best in every situation; sometimes I get it right and more often I don't, but I still think of my mistakes as stepping stones to my future. No one is perfect. However, we all have a choice in how we handle our imperfections," I voiced with confidence.
"Wow! I've never looked at it like that. Come to think about it, I guess I've always focused on my faults due to the way I felt myself. The funny thing about it – if you would have said anything like this before I started mentoring I would have never believed you. Somewhere along the way, I discovered that I was helping myself while attempting to help others. I know it sounds crazy…but no one can convince me otherwise," Lewis shared.
"Actually, it doesn't sound crazy. Honestly, it reminds me of a quote I read by Booker T. Washington a few years back – he said, 'If you want to lift yourself, lift up someone else.' That quote has never left me from the moment I heard it; and I believe it never really conveyed itself for its true meaning until now," I admitted.
"Thank you for that. That quote normalizes a lot for me. I certainly won't forget that one," Lewis added as he gazed out of the window.
"No problem, just look at my words as the echoes of others. The more we educate one another of history's truths, the more we can potentially help others with the realisms of the present and future. All of us are connected in some way or another, and it is on us to accept or decline that relationship. You've found your connection; and now you're helping others find theirs," I suggested.
As Lewis sat back in his chair, with a half-smile, he said, "And you wondered why everyone thinks you have it altogether. One day you will see what everyone else sees."
"I guess on that day we both will," I added.

I congratulated him on his engagement to-be, and he passed on his best wishes for me as well. I left *Elmer's* hoping that Lewis benefited as much as I did from our meeting and that my words would prove to be helpful beyond today.

The Great Oak

14 FRUITION

A week after Lewis headed back down South, with his "soon-to-be fiancé", and reality began to make itself well-known. The notion of the future hiding around the distant corners had proven plausible and it seemed to be awaiting a formal greeting. The day's morning minutes projected 6:00am on the alarm clock, and I rolled out of bed and my feet to hit the floor running. For the next two weeks, this would become my daily routine. I would write, edit, and taper the ideas of my literary work and brainstorm the developmental foundation of my organization. Although my efforts took away from some of the time Marie and I used to share, she offered understanding. Deep down I knew it bothered her, especially with the nuptials rapidly approaching. When I could sense any unusual level of frustration in her voice, eyes, or demeanor I would shut down my daily operations and take Marie on a "therapeutic break"; which normally entailed of a thoughtful surprise to brighten her current mood. We enjoyed activities that occupied and freed our thoughts simultaneously (e.g. karaoke, listening to live music, or the fail-safe - movie/game night without any distractions). If she seemed distant, a park, riverfront, or gazebo would soon enjoy our company; because there's nothing like communication when it comes to getting two people back on the same page.

Apart from the uncontrollable factors that are occasionally generated in the midst of several productive days, and a few moments of self-doubt, I was finally able to produce a finished product. I had already called on three different pairs of eyes to catch any grammatical or structural errors. I was expecting to get those criticisms of tough love back from my trusted sources in the upcoming week or two, so I found myself with a little free time. Since the time I accepted a buyout, four months prior, from the town's largest factory (utility appliances), getting the book published and starting the organization were my full-time jobs. In my free time, I chose to help Marie with the wedding preparations. I needed to make up for all the work she did by herself. However, I would soon find out that my assistance was no longer needed; with the exception of a couple of price tags, everything was arranged and complete. How? Well, Marie and I decided to have a very small and intimate wedding ceremony comprised of immediate family members and close friends followed by a large reception for all other family members, co-workers, childhood friends, and others. Marie was great at her craft of marketing, planning, and organization. I believe almost every woman has a vision for how she envisions the day. Marie only wanted me to be part of the process to make me feel like I contributed to our day and to be able to share in the preparation together.

The days and weeks continued to say their "hello's and goodbye's with each sunrise and sunset. My personal plans of marriage, book-publishing, and organizational-grassroots either came to pass or were in full swing, I found myself sipping down a whiskey on the rocks beside my best friend on the beach enjoying our much needed honeymoon. Every current circumstance in my life was going extremely well; I had just jumped the broom, my book was awaiting a publishing deal, and the initial gathering of my literary organization was scheduled in the upcoming months. Marie and I spent the remaining week away together before our travels back home ensued. A couple of days prior to departing from our vacation, I received a call from one of my advisors informing me that I was presented an offer for a book deal. So as it turned out, I was celebrating a new life with my soul mate as well as rejoicing the beginnings of a "dream-come-true" career. I must admit…life as I knew it became much more meaningful and purpose-driven; and I didn't plan on slowing down.

Walking through the airport terminals, going through customs, and finally landing safely stateside, I checked my voicemail and retrieved a message from an individual representing *Cornerstone Publishing Incorporated*; founded by Dr. Thomas Neal. He wanted to have a sit down with me to discuss potential options for a book deal. I agreed to meet with him the following day for brunch at, *Reginald's*, bistro downtown. The meeting presented itself as a prospective avenue to a promising opportunity for my career.

Several prayers later, along with adequate consultation and conversations of advisement, I was on my way to meet Dr. Neal at *Reginald's* to converse about possibilities. On arrival I spotted Dr. Neal occupying an outside table of the restaurant. Our conversation, surprisingly, turned out to be more faith-driven than about my literature; or at least until he explained how he thought my book aligned well with his mission of self-awareness. He began to explain that he believed life was about all individuals making informative decisions about self and learning how to care, through consideration, for others. Only after this was I fully committed to a future business with him and his association. During the last 30 minutes or so of our meeting we discussed numbers, projections, expectations, distribution and obligations. After several minor adjustments, I officially joined Dr. Neal for an exclusive publishing package that would not only promote my book but endorse the vision of my reading organization. Based on the day's events, I was thankful for this opportunity and major blessing in my life.

After cruising around town and experiencing overwhelming feelings of bliss, I felt the need to stop by Marie's marketing firm to share the wonderful news. I couldn't help but acknowledge that the air I breathed felt cleaner, the sun seemed just a little brighter, and, amazingly enough, the road and streets didn't seem to have as many potholes as I was accustomed to encountering during my normal commutes across town. Once I arrived, I saw Marie and two of her colleagues entering their store front business; probably just returning from lunch. Also, on the corner of the block I saw a man peddling flowers. So before carrying on with my surprise visit I decided to buy a couple long-stemmed roses for Marie's office. The way I planned to tell Marie my news went out of the window as my excitement mounted. "I did it…book deal…I can't believe it!," I managed to mutter. Marie could only contain herself so much. While I wondered how my Casanova-like delivery failed me, we celebrated and invited the rest of the office to join in with us.

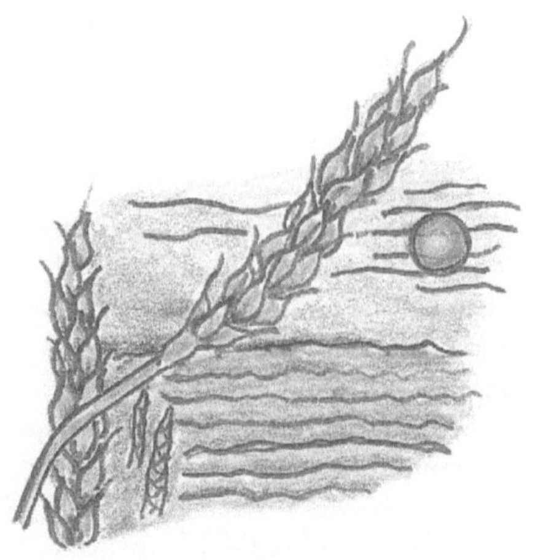

Harvest

15 THE HARVEST

Almost a year later, and I found myself speaking with one of the children involved in the reading organization about always believing in himself, when I was interrupted by Claire (my receptionist) informing me of an important phone call. I excused myself and hurried to my office to pick up line one. I picked up and recognized the stern and distinguished voice of Edwin Jacobs, a very well-known figure in the writing community. He called to inform me that there was a first-time Pulitzer Prize winner and ensured that I knew him really well.

"Is that so?," I asked.
"Do you have access to a mirror?," he asked sternly
"Yes, I do. But I'm curious…why do you ask?" I inquired.
"Well, don't worry about that right now. Just go stand in front of the mirror and let me know when you get there," he directed.
So I opened the closet door inside my office to access the full length mirror on the other side "Ok, what's the whole purpose behind this?"
"Look that person in the mirror straight in the eyes and say, 'Congratulations, you've been awarded your first Pulitzer…how does that make you feel?,'" He asked.
"Are you serious!? No way…seriously!? If this is what happens when I look

at my reflection in the mirror, I definitely need to do it more often," I jokingly replied. "But wait a minute; don't you have to be nominated for this award?" I asked.

"Yes, you do. In fact, you were nominated by a…Dr. Thomas Neal several months ago. Based on his creditability your nomination was considered, evaluated, and accepted," he responded. "Congratulations Mr. Waters, you have created a great literary work and generated a topic of many conversations to come," Jacobs stated.

"Many thanks! I'm gratefully humbled by this and I sincerely appreciate this call," I stated in return.

Over the next six months, it felt like I was living in a dream world. I could still vividly recall many sleepless and stress-filled nights of being unsure of my life's direction, or if I had even had one. And now, I'm living my life's purpose and everything seems…perfect. Due to my recent notoriety, I utilized all the contacts from my network of friends and associates to open a nation-wide reading organization in several different states tabbed *R.E.A.D.E.R.* (an abbreviation for ***R****emain* ***E****ducated* ***A****nd* ***D****on't* ***E****ver* ***R****etreat*) for all ages (K-12, College, Graduates, Parents, and Elders) where the slogan states "everyone is qualified to read."

I was on a flight to the East Coast to embark on a six week book-signing venture when a passenger, walking toward the back of the plane for what appeared to be a restroom break, recognized my face from the back cover of a new book he was reading that just happened to be entitled *Echoes of The World.* To this day, I still consider that person as the individual who prepared me for the long awaited six-week book signing endeavor. The passenger went on to explain that he was a middle-aged teacher from the southwest and how much the book had helped him reach those students he had trouble relating to before. I handed back to him an autographed copy of the book he had with him, as well as a personal business card so he could invite his students to their local *R.E.A.D.E.R.'s* facility. I used this as an opportunity to use a philosophy I've truly believed in for some time now; Reach One -Teach One. Basically, when someone reaches out to you for help or assistance – use the opportunity to teach them how to help themselves, as well as the importance of helping the next person that may reach out to them. Because all of us are part of a cycle; however, we have the choice to decide who or what we're connected to.

From city to city, and town to town, my book signing tour ensued; bringing me in contact with an array of people from very diverse cultures. Based on these observations, I had no choice but to acknowledge the underlying truth of the matter and the real purpose behind my efforts - promoting peace and social harmony. It was necessary for me to first dive into the harsh realities in which we live; by not only depicting the disparities of the world, but how we all can change if we only chose to stop and listen to the echoes of the world (or in other words…the voices of the people).

After my travels, and a few guest appearances here and there, I believe a large number of my readers and supporters really bought into the ideas and concepts presented and described in *Echoes of the World.* So much so, that I would later be awarded the Nobel Peace prize for my efforts of improving humankind through literature and the wide-spread changes accredited to the *R.E.A.D.E.R.* organization and the institution of education as a whole.

In addition it was only right that I do something in memory of my friend that would in turn help many others. Along with Chris' parents, I assisted in developing an organization called "*Open Ears*" dedicated to suicide prevention and recognizing the warning signs of suicide influenced by several journals they found that belonged to Chris. His journal entries revealed the emotional rollercoaster he was experiencing over the years that preceded his death.

Taking a retrospective glance back over my life, I'm immensely grateful for my true friends. Just think – if Lewis never mentioned starting our own reading club after I was denied access to another, and Eric, Chris, or Frank didn't support the proposal - there's a great chance none of this would have been possible. When it seems like life has locked the door to your passions, don't let it get you down. There could very well be another door around the corner waiting to be opened and bring more to you than you ever expected.

The End

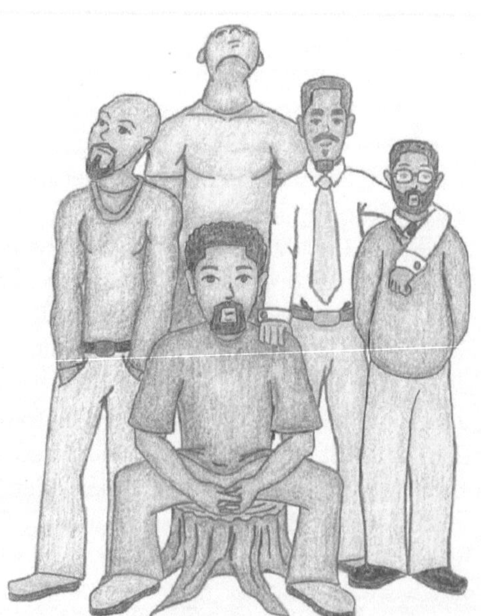

(Clockwise - Top to Bottom)
Chris Dunn
Frank Neely
Eric Thomas
James Waters
Lewis Porter

ABOUT THE AUTHOR

"I am self-motivated with the belief that there is always room for improvement and those who strive with discipline and faith will excel. I believe everyone must be a student of life; when doing so, you learn key elements required to be a leader in any field or career. Opportunities come and go, but the experience gained from each opportunity lasts forever."

~ C. J. Ward